Weapon ... or Master?

Elric brooded, and he held the black runesword
in his two hands. *Stormbringer* was more than
an ordinary battle-blade, this he had known for
years, but now he realised that it was possessed
of more sentience than he had imagined. The
frightful thing had used its wielder and had made
Elric destroy Cymoril. Yet he was horribly
dependent on it. He was an albino. Without
Stormbringer he would be slothful, his reactions
sluggish, his mind hazed. He would lose pride—
perhaps even life. But he feared and resented the
sword's power ...
Elric drew a great, sobbing breath and threw
the sword into the moon-drenched sea ...

Also available in Mayflower Books,
in the Champion Eternal series:

*Interconnected series

Michael Moorcock

The Stealer of Souls

and other stories

MAYFLOWER
GRANADA PUBLISHING
London Toronto Sydney New York

Published by Granada Publishing Limited
in Mayflower Books 1968
Reprinted 1974, 1975, 1977

ISBN 0 583 11344 3

First published in Great Britain by
Neville Spearman Ltd 1963
Copyright Michael Moorcock 1961–62
Acknowledgements
I should like to acknowledge not only
the original publication of these stories
in *Science Fantasy*, but the encouragement
and help given me when writing them by
John Carnell, the Editor. The stories originally
appeared in *Science Fantasy* issues dated
June and October 1961, and February,
August and October 1962.

Granada Publishing Limited
Frogmore, St Albans, Herts AL2 2NF
and
3 Upper James Street, London W1R 4BP
1221 Avenue of the Americas, New York, NY10020 USA
117 York Street, Sydney, NSW 2000, Australia
100 Skyway Avenue, Toronto, Ontario, Canada M9W 3A6
Trio City, Coventry Street, Johannesburg 2001, South Africa
CML Centre, Queen & Wyndham, Auckland 1, New Zealand

Made and printed in Great Britain by
Hunt Barnard Printing Ltd
Aylesbury, Bucks
Set in Monotype Times

Contents

The
Stealer
of Souls

and other stories

The Dreaming City

INTRODUCTION

FOR TEN THOUSAND years did the Bright Empire of Melniboné flourish – ruling the World. Ten thousand years before
history was recorded – or ten thousand years after history had
ceased to be chronicled. For that span of time, reckon it how
you will, the Bright Empire had thrived. Be hopeful, if you like,
and think of the dreadful past the Earth has known, or brood
upon the future. But if you would believe the unholy truth –
then Time is an agony of Now, and so it will always be.

Ravaged, at last, by the formless terror called Time,
Melniboné fell and newer nations succeeded her: Ilmiora,
Sheegoth, Maidahk, S'aaleem. Then history began: India,
China, Egypt, Assyria, Persia, Greece, and Rome – all these
came after Melniboné. But none lasted ten thousand years.

And none dealt in the terrible mysteries, the secret sorceries
of old Melniboné. None used such power or knew how. Only
Melniboné ruled the Earth for a hundred centuries – and then,
even she, shaken by the casting of frightful runes, attacked by
powers greater than men; powers who decided that Melniboné's
span of ruling had been overlong – then she crumbled and her
sons were scattered. They became wanderers across an Earth
which hated and feared them, siring few offspring, slowly dying,
slowly forgetting the secrets of their mighty ancestors. Such a
one was the cynical, laughing Elric, a man of bitter brooding
and gusty humour, proud Prince of ruins, Lord of a lost and
humbled people; last son of Melniboné's sundered line of kings.

Elric, the moody-eyed wanderer – a lonely man who fought
a world, living by his wits and his runesword *Stormbringer*.
Elric, last Lord of Melniboné, last worshipper of its grotesque
and beautiful Gods – reckless reaver and cynical slayer – torn
by great griefs and with a knowledge locked in his skull which
would turn lesser men into babbling idiots. Elric, moulder of
madnesses, dabbler in wild delights . . .

9

1

'What's the hour?' The black-bearded man wrenched off his gilded helmet and flung it from him, careless of where it fell. He drew off his leathern gauntlets and moved closer to the roaring fire, letting the heat soak into his frozen bones.

'Midnight is long past,' growled one of the other armoured men who gathered around the blaze. 'Are you still sure he'll come?'

'It's said that he's a man of his word, if that comforts you.'

It was a tall, pale-faced youth who spoke. His thin lips formed the words and spat them out maliciously. He grinned a wolf-grin and stared the new arrival in the eyes, mocking him.

The newcomer turned away with a shrug. 'That's so – for all your irony, Yaris. He'll come.' He spoke as a man does when he wishes to reassure himself.

There were six men, now, around the fire. The sixth was Smiorgan – Count Smiorgan Baldhead of the Purple Towns. He was a short, stocky man of fifty years with a scarred face partially covered with a thick, black growth of hair. His eyes smouldered morosely and his lumpy fingers plucked nervously at his rich-hilted longsword. His pate was hairless, giving him his name, and over his ornate, gilded armour hung a loose woollen cloak, dyed purple.

'For all his haughtiness and fine promises, I think Elric's our man,' Smiorgan said thickly. 'Once he gives his word, we can trust him.'

'You're full of trust tonight, Count,' Yaris smiled thinly, 'a rare thing to find in these troubled times. I say this –' He paused and took a long breath, staring at his comrades, summing them up. His gaze flicked from lean-faced Dharmit of Jharkor to Fadan of Lormyr who pursed his podgy lips and looked into the fire.

'Speak up, Yaris,' petulantly urged the patrician-featured Vilmirian, Naclon. 'Let's hear what you have to say, lad, if it's worth hearing.'

Yaris looked towards Jiku the dandy, who yawned impolitely and scratched his long nose.

'Well!' Smiorgan was impatient. 'What d'you say, Yaris?'

'I say that we should start now and waste no more time waiting on Elric's pleasure! He's laughing at us in some tavern a hundred miles from here – or else plotting with the Dragon Princes to trap us. We have little time in which to strike – our fleet is too big, too noticeable. Even if Elric has not betrayed us, then spies will soon be running eastwards to warn the Dragons that there is a fleet massed against them. We stand to win a fantastic fortune – to vanquish the greatest merchant city in the world – to reap immeasurable riches – or horrible death at the hands of the Dragon Princes, if we wait overlong. Let's bide our time no more and set sail before our prize hears of our plan and brings up reinforcements!'

'You always were too ready to mistrust a man, Yaris.' King Nalcon of Vilmir spoke slowly, carefully – distastefully eyeing the taut-featured youth. 'We could not reach Imrryr without Elric's knowledge of the maze-channels which lead to its secret ports. If Elric will not join us – then our endeavour will be fruitless – hopeless. We need him. We must wait for him – or else give up our plans and return to our homelands.'

'At least I'm willing to take a risk,' yelled Yaris, anger lancing from his slanting eyes. 'You're getting old – all of you. Treasures are not won by care and forethought but by swift slaying and reckless attack.'

'Fool!' Dharmit's voice rumbled around the fire-flooded hall. He laughed wearily. 'I spoke thus in my youth—and lost a fine fleet soon after. Cunning and Elric's knowledge will win us Imrryr – that and the mightiest fleet to sail the Sighing Sea since Melniboné's banners fluttered over all the nations of the Earth. Here we are – the most powerful Sea Lords in the world, masters, every one of us, of more than a hundred swift vessels. Our names are feared and famous – our fleets ravage the coasts of a score of lesser nations. We hold *power!*' He clenched his great fist and shook it in Yaris' face. His tone became more level and he smiled viciously, glaring at the youth and choosing his words with precision.

'But all this is worthless – meaningless – without the power which Elric has. That is the power of knowledge – of sorcery, if I must use the cursed word. His fathers knew of the maze which guards Imrryr from sea-attack. And his fathers passed that secret on to him. Imrryr, the Dreaming City, dreams in peace –

11

and will continue to do so unless we have a guide to help us steer a course through the treacherous waterways which lead to her harbours. We *need* Elric – we know it, and he knows it. That's the truth!'

'Such confidence, gentlemen, is warming to the heart.' There was laughter and irony in the voice which came from the entrance to the hall. The heads of the six Sea Lords jerked towards the doorway.

Yaris' confidence fled from him as he met the eyes of Elric of Melniboné. They were old eyes in a fine-featured, youthful face. Eyes which stared into eternity. Yaris shuddered, turned his back on Elric, preferring to look into the bright glare of the fire.

Elric smiled warmly as Count Smiorgan gripped his shoulder. There was a certain friendship between the two. He nodded condescendingly to the other four and walked with lithe grace towards the fire. Yaris stood aside and let him pass. Elric was tall, broad-shouldered and slim-hipped. He wore his long hair bunched and pinned at the nape of his neck and, for an obscure reason, affected the dress of a Southern barbarian. He had long, knee-length boots of soft doe-leather, a breastplate of strangely wrought silver, a jerkin of chequered blue and white linen, britches of scarlet wool and a cloak of rustling green velvet. At his hip rested his runesword of black iron – the feared *Stormbringer*, forged by ancient and alien sorcery when Melniboné was young.

His bizarre dress was tasteless and gaudy, and did not match his sensitive face and long-fingered, almost delicate hands, yet he flaunted it since it emphasised the fact that he did not belong in any company – that he was an outsider and an outcast. But, in reality, he had little need to wear such outlandish gear – for his face and hands were enough to mark him.

Elric, Last Lord of Melniboné, was a pure albino who drew his power from a secret and terrible source.

Smiorgan sighed. 'Well, Elric, when do we raid Imrryr?'

Elric shrugged. 'As soon as you like; I care not. Give me a ittle time in which to do certain things.'

'Tomorrow? Shall we sail tomorrow?' Yaris said hesitantly, conscious of the strange power dormant in the man he had earlier accused of treachery.

Elric smiled, dismissing the youth's statement. 'Three days' time,' he said. 'Three – or more.'

'Three days! But Imrryr will be warned of our presence by then!' Fat, cautious Fadan spoke.

'I'll see that your fleet's not found,' Elric promised. 'I have to go to Imrryr first – and return.'

'You won't do the journey in three days – the fastest ship could not make it,' Smiorgan gaped.

'I'll be in the Dreaming City in less than a day,' Elric said softly, with finality.

Smiorgan shrugged. 'If you say so, I'll believe it – but why this necessity to visit the city ahead of the raid?'

'I have my own compunctions, Count Smiorgan. But worry not – I shan't betray you. I'll lead the raid myself, be sure of that.' His dead-white face was lighted eerily by the fire and his red eyes smouldered. One lean hand firmly gripped the hilt of his runesword and he appeared to breathe more heavily. 'Imrryr fell, in spirit, five hundred years ago – she will fall completely soon – for ever! I have a little debt to settle. This is my only reason for aiding you. As you know I have made only a few conditions – that you raze the city to the ground and a certain man and woman are not harmed. I refer to my cousin Yyrkoon and his sister Cymoril . . . '

Yaris' thin lips felt uncomfortably dry. Much of his blustering manner resulted from the early death of his father. The old sea-king had died – leaving young Yaris as the new ruler of his lands and his fleets. Yaris was not at all certain that he was capable of commanding such a vast kingdom – and tried to appear more confident than he actually felt. Now he said: 'How shall we hide the fleet, Lord Elric?'

The Melnibonéan acknowledged the question. 'I'll hide it for you,' he promised. 'I go now to do this – but make sure all your men are off the ships first – will you see to it, Smiorgan?'

'Aye,' rumbled the stocky count.

He and Elric departed from the hall together, leaving five men behind; five men who sensed an air of icy doom hanging about the overheated hall.

'How could he hide such a mighty fleet when we, who know this fjord better than any, could find nowhere?' Dharmit of Jharkor said bewilderedly.

None answered him.

They waited, tensed and nervous, while the fire flickered and died untended. Eventually Smiorgan returned, stamping noisily on the boarded floor. There was a haunted haze of fear surrounding him; an almost tangible aura, and he was shivering terribly. Tremendous, racking undulations swept up his body and his breath came short.

'Well? Did Elric hide the fleet – all at once? What did he do?' Dharmit spoke impatiently, choosing not to heed Smiorgan's ominous condition.

'He has hidden it.' That was all Smiorgan said, and his voice was thin, like that of a sick man, weak from fever.

Yaris went to the entrance and tried to stare beyond the fjord slopes where many campfires burned, tried to make out the outlines of ships' masts and rigging, but he could see nothing.

'The night mist's too thick,' he murmured, 'I can't tell whether our ships are anchored in the fjord or not.' Then he gasped involuntarily as a white face loomed out of the clinging fog. 'Greetings, Lord Elric,' he stuttered, noting the sweat on the Melnibonéan's strained features.

Elric staggered past him, into the hall. 'Wine,' he mumbled, 'I've done what's needed and it's cost me hard.'

Dharmit fetched a jug of strong Cadsandrian wine and with a shaking hand poured some into a carved wooden goblet. Wordlessly he passed the cup to Elric who quickly drained it. 'Now I will sleep,' he said, stretching himself into a chair and wrapping his green cloak around him. He closed his disconcerting crimson eyes and fell into a slumber born of utter weariness.

Fadan scurried to the door, closed it and pulled the heavy iron bar down.

None of the six slept much that night and, in the morning, the door was unbarred and Elric was missing from the chair. When they went outside, the mist was so heavy that they soon lost sight of one another, though scarcely two feet separated any of them.

Elric stood with his legs astraddle on the shingle of the narrow beach. He looked back at the entrance to the fjord and saw, with satisfaction, that the mist was still thickening, though

14

it lay only over the fjord itself, hiding the mighty fleet. Elsewhere, the weather was clear and overhead a pale winter sun shone sharply on the black rocks of the rugged cliffs which dominated the coastline. Ahead of him the sea rose and fell monotonously, like the chest of a sleeping water-giant, grey and pure, glinting in the cold sunlight. Elric fingered the raised runes on the hilt of his black broadsword and a steady north wind blew into the voluminous folds of his dark green cloak, swirling it around his tall, lean frame.

The albino felt fitter than he had done on the previous night when he had expended all his strength in conjuring the mist. He was well-versed in the art of nature-wizardry, but he did not have the reserves of power which the Sorcerer Emperors of Melniboné had possessed when they had ruled the world. His ancestors had passed their knowledge down to him – but not their mystic vitality and many of the spells and secrets that he had were unusable, since he did not have the reservoir of strength, either of soul or of body, to work them. But for all that, Elric knew of only one other man who matched his knowledge – his cousin Yyrkoon. His hand gripped the hilt tighter as he thought of his cousin and he forced himself to concentrate on his present task – the speaking of spells to aid him on his voyage to the Isle of the Dragon Masters whose only city, Imrryr the Beautiful, was the object of the Sea Lords' massing.

Drawn up on the beach, a tiny sailing-boat lay – Elric's own small ship, sturdy and far stronger, far older, than it appeared. The brooding sea flung surf around its timbers as the tide withdrew, and Elric realised that he had little time in which to work his helpful sorcery.

His body tensed and he blanked his conscious mind, summoning secrets from the dark depths of his soul. Swaying, his eyes staring unseeingly, his arms jerking out ahead of him and making unholy signs in the air, he began to speak in a sibilant monotone. Slowly the pitch of his voice rose, resembling the scarcely heard shriek of a distant gale as it comes closer – then, quite suddenly, the voice rose higher until it was howling wildly to the skies and the air began to tremble and quiver. Shadow-shapes began slowly to form and they were never still but darted around Elric's body as, stiff-legged, he started forward towards his boat.

15

His voice was inhuman as it howled insistently, summoning the wind elementals – the *sylphs* of the breeze; the *sharnahs*, makers of gales; the *h'Haarshanns*, builders of whirlwinds – hazy and formless, they eddied around him as he summoned their aid with the alien words of his forefathers who had, ages before, made unthinkable pacts with the elementals in order to procure their services.

Still stiff-limbed, Elric entered the boat and, like an automaton, his fingers ran up the sail and set it. Then a great wave erupted out of the placid sea, rising higher and higher until it towered over the vessel. With a surging crash, the water smashed down on the boat, lifted it and bore it out to sea. Sitting blank-eyed in the stern, Elric still crooned his hideous song of sorcery as the spirits of the air plucked at the sail and sent the boat flying over the water faster than any mortal ship could speed. And all the while, the deafening, unholy shriek of the released elementals filled the air about the boat as the shore vanished and open sea was all that was visible.

2

So it was, with wind-demons for shipmates, that Elric, last Prince of the Royal line of Melniboné, returned to the last city still ruled by his own race – the last city and the final remnant of Melnibonéan architecture. The cloudy pink and subtle yellow tints of her nearer towers came into sight within a few hours of Elric's leaving the fjord and just off-shore of the Isle of the Dragon Masters the elementals left the boat and fled back to their secret haunts among the peaks of the highest mountains in the world. Elric awoke, then, from his trance, and regarded with fresh wonder the beauty of his own city's delicate towers which were visible even so far away, guarded still by the formidable sea-wall with its great gate, the five-doored maze and the twisting, high-walled channels, of which only one led to the inner harbour of Imrryr.

Elric knew that he dare not risk entering the harbour by the maze, though he knew the route perfectly. He decided, instead, to land the boat farther up the coast in a small inlet of which he had knowledge. With sure, capable hands, he guided the little craft towards the hidden inlet which was obscured by a

16

growth of shrubs loaded with ghastly blue berries of a type decidedly poisonous to men, since their juice first turned one blind and then slowly mad. This berry, the *nodoil*, grew only on Imrryr as did other rare and deadly plants.

Light, low-hanging cloud wisps streamed slowly across the sun-painted sky, like fine cobwebs caught by a sudden breeze. All the world seemed blue and gold and green and white, and Elric, pulling his boat up on the beach, breathed the clean, sharp air of winter and savoured the scent of decaying leaves and rotting undergrowth. Somewhere a bitch-fox barked her pleasure to her mate and Elric regretted the fact that his depleted race no longer appreciated natural beauty, preferring to stay close to their city and spend many of their days in drugged slumber. It was not the city which dreamed, but its over-civilised inhabitants. Elric smelling the rich, clean winter-scents, was wholly glad that he had renounced his birthright and did not rule the city as he had been born to do.

Instead, Yyrkoon, his cousin, sprawled on the Ruby Throne of Imrryr the Beautiful and hated Elric because he knew that the albino, for all his disgust with crowns and rulership, was still the rightful King of the Dragon Isle and that he, Yyrkoon, was an usurper, not elected by Elric to the throne and thus an illegal king by Melnibonéan tradition.

But Elric had better reasons for hating his cousin. Far better reasons. For those reasons Imrryr, the Isle's ancient capital, would fall in all its magnificent splendour and the last outpost of a glorious Empire would be obliterated as the pink, the yellow, the purple and white towers crumbled – if Elric had his way and the Sea Lords were successful.

On foot, Elric strode inland, towards Imrryr, and as he covered the miles of soft turf, the sun cast an ochre pall over the land and sank, giving way to a dark and moonless night, brooding and full of evil portent.

At last he came to the city. It stood out in stark black silhouette, a city of fantastic magnificence, in conception and in execution. It was the oldest city in the world, built by artists and conceived as a work of art rather than a functional dwelling place, but Elric knew that squalor lurked in many narrow streets and that the Lords of Imrryr, the Dragon Masters, of whom he was one, left many of the towers empty and uninhabited rather than let the bastard population of the city dwell therein. There were few Dragon Masters left; few who could claim Melnibonéan blood.

Built to follow the shape of the ground, the city had an organic appearance, with winding lanes mounting like a chord of music up to the crest of the hill where stood the castle, tall and proud and many-spired, the final, crowning masterpiece of the ancient, forgotten artist who had built it. But there was no life-sound emanating from Imrryr the Beautiful, only a sense of soporific desolation. The city slept – and the Dragon Masters and their ladies and their special slaves dreamed drug-induced dreams of grandeur and incredible horror while the rest of the population, ordered by curfew, tossed on tawdry mattresses and tried not to dream of their squalid misery.

Elric, his hand ever near his sword-hilt, slipped through an unguarded gate in the city wall and began to walk cautiously through the unlighted streets, moving upwards, through the winding lanes, towards Yyrkoon's great palace.

Wind sighed through the empty rooms of the Dragon towers and sometimes Elric would have to withdraw into places where the shadows were deeper when he heard the tramp of feet and a group of guardsmen would pass, their duty being to see that the curfew was rigidly obeyed. Often he would hear wild laughter echoing from one of the few towers still occupied, still ablaze with bright torchlight which flung strange, disturbing shadows on the walls, often, too, he would hear a chilling scream and a frenzied, idiot's yell as some wretch of a slave died in obscene agony to please his master.

Elric was not appalled by the sounds and the dim sights. He appreciated them, and sometimes he would smile maliciously upon hearing a death-scream. He was a Melnibonéan. To his mind that gave him the right to enjoy what would shock lesser mortals. He was still a Melnibonéan – their rightful leader if he chose to resume his powers of kingship – and though he had a lonely, obscure urge to wander and sample the less sophisticated pleasures of the outside world, ten thousand years of a cruel, brilliant and malicious culture was behind him and the pulse of his ancestry beat strongly in his deficient veins. He was a sorcerer and had shed blood in many devious ways in pursuit of his art.

Elric knocked impatiently upon the heavy, blackwood door. He had reached the palace and now stood by a small back entrance, glancing cautiously around him, for he knew that Yyrkoon had given the guards orders to slay him if he entered Imrryr.

A bolt squealed on the other side of the door and it moved silently inwards. A thin, seamed face fronted Elric.

'Is it the king?' whispered the man, peering out into the night. He was a tall, extremely thin individual with long, knobbly arms and legs which shifted awkwardly as he moved nearer, straining his beady eyes to get a glimpse of Elric.

'It's Prince Elric,' the albino said. 'But you forget, Tanglebones, my friend, that a new king sits on the Ruby Throne.'

Tanglebones shook his head and his sparse hair fell over his face. With a jerking movement he brushed it back and stood aside for Elric to enter. 'The Dragon Isle has but one king – and his name is Elric, whatever usurper would have it otherwise.'

Elric ignored this statement, but he smiled thinly and waited for the man to push the bolt back into place.

'She still sleeps, sire,' Tanglebones murmured as he climbed unlit stairs, Elric behind him.

'I guessed that,' Elric said. 'I do not underestimate my good cousin's powers of sorcery.'

Upwards, now, in silence, the two men climbed until at last they reached a corridor which was aflare with dancing torchlight. The marble walls reflected the flames whitely and showed Elric, crouching with Tanglebones behind a pillar, that the room in which he was interested was guarded by a massive archer – a eunuch by the look of him – who was alert and wakeful. The man was hairless and fat, his blue-black gleaming armour tight on his flesh, but his fingers were curled around the string of his short, bone bow and there was a slim arrow resting on the string. Elric guessed that this man was one of the crack eunuch archers, a member of the Silent Guard, Imrryr's finest company of warriors.

Tanglebones, who had taught the young Elric the arts of fencing and archery, had known of the guard's presence and had prepared for it. Earlier he had placed a bow behind the pillar. Silently he picked it up and, bending it against his knee, strung it. He fitted an arrow to the string, aimed it at the right eye of the guard and let fly – just as the eunuch turned to face him. The shaft missed. It clattered against the man's gorget and fell harmlessly to the reed-strewn stones of the floor.

So Elric acted swiftly, leaping forward, his runesword drawn and its alien power surging through him. It howled in a searing arc of black steel and cut through the bone bow which the eunuch had hoped would deflect it. The guard was panting and his thick lips were wet as he drew breath to yell. As he opened his mouth, Elric saw what he had expected, the man was tongueless and was a mute. His own shortsword came out and he just managed to parry Elric's next thrust. Sparks flew from the iron and *Stormbringer* bit into the eunuch's finely edged blade, he staggered and fell back before the nigromantic sword which appeared to be endowed with a life of its own. The clatter of metal echoed loudly up and down the short corridor and Elric cursed the fate which had made the man turn at the crucial moment. Grimly, swiftly, he broke down the eunuch's clumsy guard.

The eunuch saw only a dim glimpse of his opponent behind the black, whirling blade which appeared to be so light and which was twice the length of his now stabbing sword. He wondered, frenziedly, who his attacker could be and he thought he recognised the face. Then a scarlet eruption obscured his vision, he felt searing agony clutch at his face and then, philosophically, for eunuchs are necessarily given to a certain fatalism, he realised that he was to die.

Elric stood over the eunuch's bloated body and tugged his sword from the corpse's skull, wiping the mixture of blood and brains on his late opponent's cloak. Tanglebones had wisely vanished. Elric could hear the clatter of sandalled feet rushing up the stairs. He pushed the door open and entered the room which was lit by two small candles placed at either end of a wide, richly tapestried bed. He went to the bed and looked down at the raven-haired girl who lay there.

Elric's mouth twitched and bright tears leapt into his strange red eyes. He was trembling as he turned back to the door, sheathed his sword and pulled the bolts into place. He returned to the bedside and knelt down beside the sleeping girl. Her features were as delicate and of a similar mould as Elric's own, but she had an added, exquisite beauty. She was breathing shallowly, in a sleep induced not by natural weariness but by her own brother's evil sorcery.

Elric reached out and tenderly took one fine-fingered hand in his. He put it to his lips and kissed it.

'Cymoril,' he murmured, and there was an agony of longing throbbing in that single name. 'Cymoril – wake up.'

The girl did not stir, her breathing remained shallow and her eyes remained shut. Elric's white features twisted and his red eyes blazed as he shook in terrible and passionate rage. He gripped the hand, so limp and nerveless, like the hand of a corpse; gripped it until he had to stop himself for fear that he would crush the delicate fingers.

A shouting soldier began to beat at the door.

Elric replaced the hand on the girl's firm breast and stood up. He glanced uncomprehendingly at the door.

A sharper, colder voice interrupted the soldier's yelling.

'What is happening – has someone tried to see my poor sleeping sister?'

'Yyrkoon, the black hellspawn,' said Elric to himself.

Confused babblings from the soldier and Yyrkoon's voice raised as he shouted through the door. "Whoever is in there – you will be destroyed a thousand times when you are caught. You cannot escape. If my good sister is harmed in any way – then you will never die, I promise you that. But you will pray to your Gods that you could!'

'Yyrkoon, you paltry rabble – you cannot threaten one who is your equal in the dark arts. It is I, Elric – your rightful master. Return to your rabbit hole before I call down every evil power upon, above, and under the Earth to blast you!'

Yyrkoon laughed hesitantly. 'So you have returned again to try and awake my sister have you, Elric?' he replied. 'You will never succeed – only I possess the knowledge which will awaken her. Any attempt to do so on your part will not only slay her – it will send her soul into the deepest hell – where you may join it, willingly!'

'You offspring of a festering worm, Yyrkoon. You'll have cause to repent this vile spell before your time is run! If you think you can stop Cymoril and I loving one another by a sleeping potion – then you are more than the babbling fool I know you to be! By Arnara's six breasts, I swear to you – you it will be who samples the thousand deaths before long.'

'Enough of this,' answered Yyrkoon. 'Soldiers – I command you to break this door down – and take the scum in there alive. Elric – there are two things you will never again have, this *I* swear to you – my sister's love and the Ruby Throne. Make what you can of the little time available to you, for soon you will be grovelling to me and praying for release from the agony your soul will experience.'

Elric ignored Yyrkoon's threats and looked at the narrow window to the room. It was just large enough for a man's body to pass through. He bent down and kissed Cymoril upon the lips, then he went to the door and silently withdrew the bolts.

There came a crash as a soldier flung his weight against the door. It swung open, pitching the man forward to stumble and fall on his face. Elric drew his sword, lifted it high and chopped at the warrior's neck. The head sprang from its shoulders and Elric yelled loudly in a deep, rolling voice.

'*Arioch! Arioch!* I give you blood and souls – only aid me now! This man I give you, mighty King of Hell – aid your servant, Elric of Melniboné!'

Three soldiers entered the room in a bunch. Elric struck at one and sheared off half his face. The man screamed horribly.

'Arioch, Lord of the Darks – I give you blood and souls. Aid me, evil one!'

In the far corner of the gloomy room, a blacker mist began, slowly, to form. But the soldiers pressed closer and Elric was hard put to hold them back.

He was screaming the name of Arioch, Lord of the Higher Hell, incessantly, almost unconsciously as he was pressed back further by the weight of the warriors' numbers. Behind them, Yyrkoon mouthed in rage and frustration, urging his men, still, to take Elric alive. This necessity gave Elric some small advantage – that and the runesword *Stormbringer* which was glowing with a strange black luminousness and the shrill howling it gave out was grating into the ears of those who heard it. Two more corpses now littered the carpeted floor of the chamber, their blood soaking into the fine fabric.

'*Blood and souls for my lord Arioch!*'

The dark mist heaved and began to take shape, Elric spared a look towards the corner and shuddered despite his inurement to hell-born horror. The warriors how had their backs to the thing in the corner and Elric was by the window. The amorphous mass heaved again and Elric made out its intolerably alien shape. Bile flooded into his mouth and as he drove the soldiers towards the thing which was sinuously flooding forward he fought against madness.

Suddenly, the soldiers seemed to sense that there was something behind them. They turned, four of them, and each screamed insanely as the black horror made one final rush to engulf them. Arioch crouched over them, sucking out their souls. Then, slowly, their bones began to give and snap and still shrieking bestially the men flopped like obnoxious invertebrates upon the floor; their spines broken, they still lived. Elric turned away, thankful for once that Cymoril slept, and leapt to the window ledge. He looked down and realised with despair that he was not going to escape by that route after all. Several hundred feet lay between him and the ground. He rushed to the door where Yyrkoon, his eyes wide with fear, was trying to drive Arioch back to the slime from which he had come. And he was succeeding.

Elric pushed past his cousin, spared a final glance for Cymoril, then ran back the way he had come, his feet slipping on blood. Tanglebones met him at the head of the dark stairway.

'What has happened, King Elric – what's in there?'

Elric seized Tanglebones by his lean shoulder and made him descend the stairs. 'No time,' he panted, 'but we must hurry while Yyrkoon is still engaged with his current problem. In five days' time Imrryr will experience a new phase in her history – perhaps the last. I want you to make sure that Cymoril is safe. Is that clear?'

'Aye, Lord, but . . . '

They reached the door and Tanglebones shot the bolts and opened it.

'There is no time for me to say anything else. I must escape while I can. I will return in five days – with companions. You will realise what I mean when that time comes. Take Cymoril to the Tower of D'a'rputna – and await me there.'

Then Elric was gone, soft-footed, running into the night with the shrieks of the dying still ringing through the blackness after him.

Elric stood unspeaking in the prow of Count Smiorgan's flagship. Since his return to the fjord and the fleet's subsequent sailing for open sea, he had spoken only orders, and those in the tersest of terms. The Sea Lords muttered that a great hate lay in him, that it festered his soul and made him a dangerous man to have as comrade or enemy; and even Count Smiorgan avoided the moody albino.

The reaver prows struck eastward and the sea was black with light ships dancing on the bright water in all directions; they looked like the shadow of some enormous sea-bird flung on the water. Nearly half a thousand fighting ships stained the ocean – all of them of similar form, long and slim and built for speed rather than battle, since they were for coast-raiding and trading. Sails were caught by the pale sun; bright colours of fresh canvas – orange, blue, black, purple, red, yellow, light green or white. And every ship had sixteen or more rowers – each rower a fighting man. The crews of the ships were also the warriors who would attack Imrryr – there was no wastage of good man-power since the sea-nations were underpopulated, losing hundreds of men each year in their regular raids.

In the centre of the great fleet, certain larger vessels sailed. These carried great catapults on their decks and were to be used for storming the sea wall of Imrryr. Count Smiorgan and the other Lords looked at their ships with pride, but Elric only stared ahead of him, never sleeping, rarely moving, his white face lashed by salt spray and wind, his white hand tight upon his swordhilt.

The reaver ships ploughed steadily eastwards – forging towards the Dragon Isle and fantastic wealth – or hellish horror. Relentlessly, doom-driven, they beat onwards, their oars plashing in unison, their sails bellying taut with a good wind.

Onwards they sailed, towards Imrryr the Beautiful, to rape and plunder the world's oldest city.

Two days after the fleet had set sail, the coastline of the Dragon Isle was sighted and the rattle of arms replaced the sound of oars as the mighty fleet hove to and prepared to accomplish what sane men thought impossible.

Orders were bellowed from ship to ship and the fleet began to mass into battle formation; then the oars creaked in their grooves and ponderously, with sails now furled, the fleet moved forward again.

It was a clear day, cold and fresh, and there was a tense excitement about all the men, from Sea Lord to galley hand, as they considered the immediate future and what it might bring. Serpent prows bent towards the great stone wall which blocked off the first entrance to the harbour. It was nearly a hundred feet high and towers were built upon it – more functional than the lace-like spires of the city which shimmered in the distance, behind them. The ships of Imrryr were the only vessels allowed to pass through the great gate in the centre of the wall and the route through the maze – the exact entrance even – was a well-kept secret from outsiders.

On the sea wall, which now loomed tall above the fleet, amazed guards scrambled frantically to their posts. To them, threat of attack was well-nigh unthinkable, yet here it was – a great fleet, the greatest they had ever seen – come against Imrryr the Beautiful! They took to their posts, their yellow cloaks and kilts rustling, their bronze armour rattling, but they moved with bewildered reluctance as if refusing to accept what they saw. And they went to their posts with desperate fatalism, knowing that even if the ships never entered the maze itself, they would not be alive to witness the reavers' failure.

Dyvim Tarkan, Commander of the Wall, was a sensitive man who loved life and its pleasures. He was highbrowed and handsome, with a thin wisp of beard and a tiny moustache. He looked well in the bronze armour and high-plumed helmet; he did not want to die. He issued terse orders to his men and, with well-ordered precision, they obeyed him. He listened with concern to the distant shouts from the ships and he wondered what the first move of the reavers would be. He did not wait long for his answer.

A catapult on one of the leading vessels twanged throatily and its throwing arm rushed up, releasing a great rock which sailed, with every appearance of calm grace, towards the wall. It fell short and splashed into the sea which frothed against the stones of the wall.

Swallowing hard and trying to control the shake in his voice, Dyvim Tarkan ordered his own catapult to discharge. With a thudding crash the release rope was cut and a retaliatory iron ball went hurtling towards the enemy fleet. So tight-packed were the ships that the ball could not miss – it struck full on the deck of the flagship of Dharmit of Jharkor and crushed the timbers in. Within seconds, accompanied by the cries of maimed and drowning men, the ship had sunk and Dharmit with it. Some of the crew were taken aboard other vessels but the wounded were left to drown.

Another catapult sounded and this time a tower full of archers was squarely hit. Masonry erupted outwards and those who still lived fell sickeningly to die in the foam-tipped sea lashing the wall. This time, angered by the deaths of their comrades, Imrryrian archers sent back a stream of slim arrows into the enemy's midst. Reavers howled as red-fletched shafts buried themselves thirstily in flesh. But reavers returned the arrows liberally and soon only a handful of men were left on the wall as further catapult rocks smashed into towers and men, destroying their only war-machine and part of the wall besides.

Dyvim Tarkan still lived, though red blood stained his yellow tunic and an arrow shaft protruded from his left shoulder. He still lived when the first ram-ship moved intractably towards the great wooden gate and smashed against it, weakening it. A second ship sailed in beside it and, between them, they stove in the gate and glided through the entrance; the first non-Imrryrian ships ever to do such a thing. Perhaps it was outraged horror that tradition had been broken which caused poor Dyvim Tarkan to lose his footing at the edge of the wall and fall screaming down to break his neck on the deck of Count Smiorgan's flagship as it sailed triumphantly through the gate.

Now the ram-ships made way for Count Smiorgan's craft, for Elric had to lead the way though the maze. Ahead of them loomed five tall entrances, black gaping maws all alike in shape and size. Elric pointed to the third from the left and with short strokes the oarsmen began to paddle the ship into the dark mouth of the entrance. For some minutes, they sailed in darkness.

'Flares!' shouted Elric. 'Light the flares!'

Torches had already been prepared and these were now lighted. The men saw that they were in a vast tunnel hewn out of natural rock which twisted tortuously in all directions.

'Keep close,' Elric ordered and his voice was magnified a score of times in the echoing cavern. Torchlight blazed and Elric's face was a mask of shadow and frisking light as the torches threw up long tongues of flame to the bleak roof. Behind him, men could be heard muttering in awe and, as more craft entered the maze and lit their own torches, Elric could see some torches waver as their bearers trembled in superstitious fear. Elric felt some discomfort as he glanced through the flickering shadows and his eyes, caught by torchflare, gleamed fever-bright.

With dreadful monotony, the oars splashed onwards as the tunnel widened and several more cave-mouths came into sight. 'The middle entrance,' Elric ordered. The steersman in the stern nodded and guided the ship towards the entrance Elric had indicated. Apart from the muted murmur of some men and the splash of oars, there was a grim and ominous silence in the towering cavern.

Elric stared down at the cold, dark water and shuddered.

Eventually they moved once again into bright sunlight and the men looked upwards, marvelling at the height of the great walls above them. Upon those walls squatted more yellow-clad, bronze-armoured archers and as Count Smiorgan's vessel led the way out of the black caverns, the torches still burning in the cool winter air, arrows began to hurtle down into the narrow canyon, biting into throats and limbs.

'Faster!' howled Elric. 'Row faster – speed must be our only weapon now!'

With frantic energy the oarsmen bent to their sweeps and the ships began to pick up speed even though Imrryrian arrows took heavy toll of the reaver crewmen. Now the high-walled channel ran straight and Elric saw the quays of Imrryr ahead of him.

'*Faster! Faster! Our prize is in sight!*'

Then, suddenly, the ship broke past the walls and was in the calm waters of the harbour, facing the warriors drawn up on the quay. The ship halted, waiting for reinforcements to plunge out of the channel and join them. When twenty ships were

27

through, Elric gave the command to attack the quay and now *Stormbringer* howled from its scabbard. The flagship's port side thudded against the quay as arrows rained down upon it. Shafts whistled all around Elric but, miraculously, he was unscathed as he led a bunch of yelling reavers on to land. Imrryrian axe-men bunched forward and confronted the reavers, but it was plain that they had little spirit for the fight – they were too disconcerted by the course which events had taken.

Elric's black blade struck with frenzied force at the throat of the leading axe-man and sheared off his head. Howling demoniacally now that it had again tasted blood, the sword began to writhe in Elric's grasp, seeking fresh flesh in which to bite. There was a hard, grim smile on the albino's colourless lips and his eyes were narrowed as he struck without discrimination at the warriors.

He planned to leave the fighting to those he had led to Imrryr, for he had other things to do – and quickly. Behind the yellow-garbed soldiers, the tall towers of Imrryr rose, beautiful in their soft and scintillating colours of coral pink and powdery blue, of gold and pale yellow, white and subtle green. One such tower was Elric's objective – the tower of D'a'rputna where he had ordered Tanglebones to take Cymoril, knowing that in the confusion this would be possible.

Elric hacked a blood-drenched path through those who attempted to halt him and men fell back, screaming horribly as the runesword drank their souls.

Now Elric was past them, leaving them to the bright blades of the reavers who poured on to the quayside, and was running up through the twisting streets, his sword slaying anyone who attempted to stop him. Like a whitefaced ghoul he was, his clothing tattered and bloody, his armour chipped and scratched, but he ran speedily over the cobble-stones of the twisting streets and came at last to the slender tower of hazy blue and soft gold – the Tower of D'a'rputna. Its door was open, showing that someone was inside, and Elric rushed through it and entered the large ground-floor chamber. No one greeted him.

'Tanglebones!' he yelled, his voice roaring loudly even in his own ears. 'Tanglebones – are you here?' He leapt up the stairs in great bounds, calling his servant's name. On the third floor he stopped suddenly, hearing a low groan from one of the rooms. 'Tanglebones – is that you?' Elric strode towards the room, hearing a strangled gasping. He pushed open the door and his stomach seemed to twist within him as he saw the old man lying upon the bare floor of the chamber, striving vainly to stop the flow of blood which gouted from a great wound in his side.

'What's happened, man – where's Cymoril?'

Tanglebones' old face twisted in pain and grief. 'She – I – I brought her here, master, as you ordered. But – ' he coughed and blood dribbled down his wizened chin, 'but – Prince Yyrkoon – he – he apprehended me – must have followed us here. He – struck me down and took Cymoril back with him – said she'd be – safe in the Tower of B'aal'nezbett. Master – I'm sorry . . . '

'So you should be,' Elric retorted savagely. Then his tone softened. 'Do not worry, old friend – I'll avenge you and myself. I can still reach Cymoril now I know where Yyrkoon has taken her. Thank you for trying, Tanglebones – may the long journey down the last river be a safe one.'

He turned abruptly on his heel and left the chamber, running down the stairs and out into the street again.

The tower of B'aal'nezbett was the highest tower in the Royal Palace. Elric knew it well, for it was there that his ancestors had studied their dark sorceries and conducted frightful experiments. He shuddered as he thought what Yyrkoon might be doing to his own sister.

The streets of the city seemed hushed and strangely deserted, but Elric had no time to ponder why this should be so. Instead he dashed towards the palace, found the main gate unguarded and the main entrance to the building deserted. This too was unique, but it constituted luck for Elric as he made his way upwards, climbing familiar ways towards the topmost tower.

Finally, he reached a door of shimmering black crystal which had no bolt or handle to it. Frenziedly, Elric struck at the crystal with his sorcerous blade but the crystal appeared only to flow and re-form. His blows had no effect.

Elric racked his mind, seeking to remember the single alien word which would make the door open. He dare not put himself in the trance which would have, in time, brought the word to his lips, instead he had to dredge his subconscious and bring

29

the word forth. It was dangerous but there was little else he could do. His whole frame trembled as his face twisted and his brain began to shake. The word was coming as his vocal chords jerked in his throat and his chest heaved.

He coughed the word out and his whole mind and body ached with the strain. Then he cried:

'I command thee – open!'

He knew that once the door opened, his cousin would be aware of his presence, but he had to risk it. The crystal expanded, pulsating and seething, and then began to flow *out*. It flowed into nothingness, into something beyond the physical universe, beyond time. Elric breathed thankfully and passed into the Tower of B'aal'nezbett. But now an eerie fire, chilling and mind-shattering, was licking around Elric as he struggled up the steps towards the central chamber. There was a strange music surrounding him, uncanny music which throbbed and sobbed and pounded in his head.

Above him he saw a leering Yyrkoon, a black runesword also in his hand, the mate of the one in Elric's own grasp.

'Hellspawn!' Elric said thickly, weakly, 'I see you have recovered *Mournblade* – well, test its powers against its brother if you dare. I have come to destroy you, cousin.'

Stormbringer was giving forth a peculiar moaning sound which sighed over the shrieking, unearthly music accompanying the licking, chilling fire. The runesword writhed in Elric's fist and he had difficulty in controlling it. Summoning all his strength he plunged up the last few steps and aimed a wild blow at Yyrkoon. Beyond the eerie fire bubbled yellow-green lava, on all sides, above and beneath. The two men were surrounded only by the misty fire and the lava which lurked beyond it – they were outside the Earth and facing one another for a final battle. The lava seethed and began to ooze inwards, dispersing – not *engulfing* the fire.

The two blades met and a terrible shrieking roar went up. Elric felt his whole arm go numb and it tingled sickeningly. Elric felt like a puppet. He was no longer his own master – the blade was deciding his actions for him. The blade, with Elric behind it, roared past its brother sword and cut a deep wound in Yyrkoon's left arm. He howled and his eyes widened in agony. *Mournblade* struck back at *Stormbringer*, catching

Elric in the very place he had wounded his cousin. He sobbed in pain, but continued to move upwards, now wounding Yyrkoon in the right side with a blow strong enough to have killed any other man. Yyrkoon laughed then – laughed like a gibbering demon from the foulest depths of Hell. His sanity had broken at last and Elric now had the advantage. But the great sorcery which his cousin had conjured was still in evidence and Elric felt as if a giant had grasped him, was crushing him as he pressed his advantage, Yyrkoon's blood spouting from the wound and covering Elric, also. The lava was slowly withdrawing and now Elric saw the entrance to the central chamber. Behind his cousin another form moved. Elric gasped. Cymoril had awakened and, with horror on her face, was shrieking at him.

The sword still swung in a black arc, cutting down Yyrkoon's brother blade and breaking the usurper's guard.

'Elric!' cried Cymoril desperately. 'Save me – save me now, else we are doomed for eternity.'

Elric was puzzled by the girl's words. He could not understand the sense of them. Savagely he drove Yyrkoon upwards towards the chamber.

'Elric – put *Stormbringer* away. Sheath your sword or we shall part again.'

But even if he could have controlled the whistling blade, Elric would not have sheathed it. Hate dominated his being and he would sheathe it in his cousin's evil heart before he put it aside.

Cymoril was weeping, now, pleading with him. But Elric could do nothing. The drooling, idiot thing which had been Yyrkoon of Imrryr, turned at its sister's cries and stared leeringly at her. It cackled and reached out one shaking hand to seize the girl by her shoulder. She struggled to escape, but Yyrkoon still had his evil strength. Taking advantage of his opponent's distraction, Elric cut deep through his body, almost severing the trunk from the waist.

And yet, incredibly, Yyrkoon remained alive, drawing his vitality from the blade which still clashed against Elric's own rune-carved sword. With a final push he flung Cymoril forward and she died screaming on the point of *Stormbringer*

Then Yyrkoon laughed one final crackling shriek and his

black soul went howling down to hell.

The tower resumed its former proportions, all fire and lava gone. Elric was dazed – unable to marshal his thoughts. He looked down at the dead bodies of the brother and the sister. He saw them, at first, only as corpses – a man's and a woman's.

Then dark truth dawned on his clearing brain and he moaned in grief, like an animal. He had slain the girl he loved. The runesword fell from his grasp, stained by Cymoril's lifeblood, and clattered unheeded down the stairs. Sobbing now, Elric dropped beside the dead girl and lifted her in his arms.

'Cymoril,' he moaned, his whole body throbbing. 'Cymoril – I have slain you.'

4

Elric looked back at the roaring, crumbling, tumbling, flame-spewing ruins of Imrryr and drove his sweating oarsmen faster. The ship, sail still unfurled, bucked as a contrary current of wind caught it and Elric was forced to cling to the ship's side lest he be tossed overboard. He looked back at Imrryr and felt a tightness in his throat as he realised that he was truly rootless, now; a renegade and a woman-slayer, though involuntarily the latter. He had lost the only woman he had loved in his blind lust for revenge. Now it was finished – everything was finished. He could envisage no future, for his future had been bound up with his past and now, effectively, that past was flaming in ruins behind him. Dry sobs eddied in his chest and he gripped the ship's rail yet more firmly.

His mind reluctantly brooded on Cymoril. He had laid her corpse upon a couch and had set fire to the Tower. Then he had gone back to find the reavers successful, straggling back to their ships loaded with loot and girl-slaves, jubilantly firing the tall and beautiful buildings as they went.

He had caused to be destroyed the last tangible sign that the grandiose, magnificent Bright Empire had ever existed. He felt that most of himself was gone with it.

Elric looked back at Imrryr and suddenly a greater sadness overwhelmed him as a tower, as delicate and as beautiful as fine lace, cracked and toppled with flames leaping about it.

He had shattered the last great monument to the earlier race –

his own race. Men might have learned again, one day, to build strong, slender towers like those of Imrryr, but now the knowledge was dying with the thundering chaos of the fall of the Dreaming City and the fast-diminishing race of Melniboné.

But what of the Dragon Masters? Neither they nor their golden ships had met the attacking reavers – only their foot-soldiers had been there to defend the city. Had they hidden their ships in some secret waterway and fled inland when the reavers overran the city? They had put up too short a fight to be truly beaten. It had been far too easy. Now that the ships were retreating, were they planning some sudden retaliation? Elric felt that they might have such a plan – perhaps a plan concerning dragons. He shuddered. He had told the others nothing of the beasts which Melnibonéans had controlled for centuries. Even now, someone might be unlocking the gates of the underground Dragon Caves. He turned his mind away from the unnerving prospect.

As the fleet headed towards open sea, Elric's eyes were still looking sadly towards Imrryr as he paid silent homage to the city of his forefathers and the dead Cymoril. He felt hot bitterness sweep over him again as the memory of her death upon his own sword-point came sharply to him. Then a muttering, like a roll of distant thunder, spread through the fleet and he wheeled sharply, intent on discovering the cause of the consternation.

Thirty golden-sailed Melnibonéan battle barges had appeared on both sides of the harbour, issuing from two mouths of the maze. Elric realised that they must have hidden in the other channels, waiting to attack the fleet when they returned, satiated and depleted. Great war-galleys they were, the last ships of Melniboné and the secret of their building was unknown. They had a sense of age and slumbering might about them as they rowed swiftly, each with four or five banks of great sweeping oars, to encircle the raven ships.

Elric's fleet seemed to shrink before his eyes until it seemed as though it were a bobbing collection of wood-shavings against the towering splendour of the shimmering battle barges. They were well-equipped and fresh for a fight, whereas the weary reavers were intensely battle-tired. There was only one way to save a small part of the fleet, Elric knew. He would have to conjure a witch-wind for sailpower. Most of the flagships were around him and he now occupied that of Yaris, for the youth had got himself wildly drunk and had died by the knife of an Imrryrian tavern wench. Next to Elric's ship was Count Smiorgan's and the stocky Sea Lord was frowning, knowing full well that he and his ships, for all their superior numbers, would not stand up to a sea-fight.

But the conjuring of winds great enough to move many vessels was a dangerous thing, for it released colossal power and the elementals who controlled the winds were apt to turn upon the sorcerer himself if he was not more than careful. But it was the only chance, otherwise the rams which sent ripples from the golden prows would smash the reaver ships to driftwood.

Steeling himself, Elric began to speak the ancient and terrible, many-vowelled names of the beings who existed in the air. Again, he could not risk the trance-state, for he had to watch for signs of the elementals' turning upon him. He called to them in a speech that was sometimes high like the cry of a gannet, sometimes rolling like the roar of shore-bound surf, and the dim shapes of the Powers of the Wind began to flit before his blurred gaze. His heart throbbed horribly in his ribs and his legs felt weak. He summoned all his strength and conjured a wind which shrieked wildly and chaotically about him, rocking even the huge Melnibonéan ships back and forth. Then he directed the wind and sent it into the sails of some forty of the reaver ships. Many he could not save for they lay even outside his wide range.

But forty of the craft escaped the smashing rams and, amidst the sound of howling wind and sundered timbers, leapt on the waves, their masts creaking as the wind cracked into their sails. Oars were torn from the hands of the rowers, leaving a wake of broken wood on the white salt trail which boiled behind each of the reaver ships.

Quite suddenly, they were beyond the slowly closing circle of Melnibonéan ships and careering madly across the open sea, while all the crews sensed a difference in the air and caught glimpses of strange, soft-shaped forms around them. There was a discomforting sense of evil about the beings which aided them, an awesome alienness.

34

Smiorgan waved to Elric and grinned thankfully.

'We're safe, thanks to you, Elric!' he yelled across the water. 'I knew you'd bring us luck!'

Elric ignored him.

Now the Dragon Lords, vengeance-bent, gave chase. Almost as fast as the magic-aided reaver fleet were the golden barges of Imrryr, and some reaver galleys, whose masts cracked and split beneath the force of the wind driving them, were caught.

Elric saw mighty grapple-hooks of dully gleaming metal swing out from the decks of the Imrryrian galleys and thud with a moan of wrenched timber into those of the fleet which lay broken and powerless behind him. Greek fire leapt from catapults upon the Dragon Lords' ships and careered towards many a fleeing reaver craft. Searing, foul-stinking flame hissed like lava across the decks and ate into planks like vitriol into paper. Men shrieked, beating vainly at brightly burning clothes, some leaping into water which would not extinguish the fire. Some sank beneath the sea and it was possible to trace their descent as, flaming even below the surface, men and ships fluttered to the bottom like blazing, tired moths.

Reaver decks, untouched by fire, ran red with reaver blood as the enraged Imrryrian warriors swung down the grappling ropes and dropped among the raiders, wielding great swords and battle-axes and wreaking terrible havoc amongst the sea-ravens. Imrryrian arrows and Imrryrian javelins swooped from the towering decks of Imrryrian galleys and tore into the panicky men on the smaller ships.

All this Elric saw as he and his vessels began slowly to overhaul the leading Imrryrian ship, flag-galley of Admiral Magum Colim, commander of the Melnibonéan fleet.

Now Elric spared a word for Count Smiorgan. 'We've outrun them!' he shouted above the howling wind to the next ship where Smiorgan stood staring wide-eyed at the sky. 'But keep your ships heading westwards or we're finished!'

But Smiorgan did not reply. He still looked skyward and there was horror in his eyes; in the eyes of a man who, before this, had never known the quivering bite of fear. Uneasily, Elric let his own eyes follow the gaze of Smiorgan. Then he saw them.

They were dragons, without doubt! The great reptiles were

35

some miles away, but Elric knew the stamp of the huge flying beasts. The average wingspan of these near-extinct monsters was some thirty feet across. Their snakelike bodies, beginning in a narrow-snouted head and terminating in a dreadful whip of a tail, were forty feet long and although they did not breathe the legendary fire and smoke, Elric knew that their venom was combustible and could set fire to wood or fabric on contact.

Imrryrian warriors rode the dragon backs. Armed with long, spear-like goads, they blew strangely shaped horns which sang out curious notes over the turbulent sea and calm blue sky. Nearing the golden fleet, now half-a-league away, the leading dragon sailed down and circled towards the huge golden flag-galley, its wings making a sound like the crack of lightning as they beat through the air.

The grey-green, scaled monster hovered over the golden ship as it heaved in the white-foamed turbulent sea. Framed against the cloudless sky, the dragon was in sharp perspective and it was possible for Elric to get a clear view of it. The goad which the Dragon Master waved to Admiral Magum Colim was a long, slim spear upon which the strange pennant of black and yellow zigzag lines was, even at this distance, noticeable. Elric recognized the insignia on the pennant.

Dyvim Tvar, friend of Elric's youth, Lord of the Dragon Caves, was leading his charges to claim vengeance for Imrryr the Beautiful.

Elric howled across the water to Smiorgan. 'These are your main danger, now. Do what you can to stave them off!' There was a rattle of iron as the men prepared, near-hopelessly, to repel the new menace. Witch-wind would give little advantage over the fast-flying dragons. Now Dyvim Tvar had evidently conferred with Magum Colim and his goad lashed out at the dragon throat. The huge reptile jerked upwards and began to gain altitude. Eleven other dragons were behind it, joining it now.

With seeming slowness, the dragons began to beat relentlessly towards the reaver fleet as the crewmen prayed to their own Gods for a miracle.

They were doomed. There was no escaping the fact. Every reaver ship was doomed and the raid had been fruitless.

Elric could see the despair in the faces of the men as the

masts of the reaver ships continued to bend under the strain of the shrieking witch-wind. They could do nothing, now, but die . . .

Elric fought to rid his mind of the swirling uncertainty which filled it. He drew his sword and felt the pulsating, evil power which lurked in rune-carved *Stormbringer*. But he hated that power now – for it had caused him to kill the only human he had cherished. He realised how much of his strength he owed to the black-iron sword of his fathers and how weak he might be without it. He was an albino and that meant that he lacked the vitality of a normal human being. Savagely, futilely, as the mist in his mind was replaced by red fear, he cursed the pretensions of revenge he had held, cursed the day when he had agreed to lead the raid on Imrryr and most of all he bitterly vilified dead Yyrkoon and his twisted envy which had been the cause of the whole doom-ridden course of events.

But it was too late, now, for curses of any kind. The loud slapping of beating dragon wings filled the air and the monsters loomed over the fleeing reaver craft. He had to make some kind of decision – though he had no love for life, he refused to die by the hands of his own people. When he died, he promised himself, it would be by his own hand. He made his decision, hating himself.

He called off the witch-wind as the dragon venom seared down and struck the last ship in line.

He put all his powers into sending a stronger wind into the sails of his own boat while his bewildered comrades in the suddenly becalmed ships called over the water, inquiring desperately the reason for his act. Elric's ship was moving fast, now, and might just escape the dragons. He hoped so.

He deserted the man who had trusted him, Count Smiorgan, and watched as venom poured from the sky and engulfed him in blazing green and scarlet flame. Elric fled, keeping his mind from thoughts of the future, and sobbed aloud, that proud prince of ruins; and he cursed the malevolent Gods for the black day when idly, for their amusement, they had spawned men.

Behind him, the last reaver ships flared into sudden appalling brightness and, although half-thankful that they had escaped the fate of their comrades, the crew looked at Elric accusingly.

He sobbed on, not heeding them, great griefs racking his soul.

A night later, off the coast of an island called Pan Tang, when the ship was safe from the dreadful recriminations of the Dragon Masters and their beasts, Elric stood brooding in the stern while the men eyed him with fear and hatred, muttering of betrayal and heartless cowardice. They appeared to have forgotten their own fear and subsequent safety.

Elric brooded, and he held the black runesword in his two hands. *Stormbringer* was more than an ordinary battle-blade, this he had known for years, but now he realised that it was possessed of more sentience than he had imagined. The frightful thing had used its wielder and had made Elric destroy Cymoril. Yet he was horribly dependent upon it; he realised this with soul-rending certainty. He was an albino – a type rare among animals and rarer still among men. He was an albino, owning no natural reserves of vitality. Normally, he would be slothful, his reactions sluggish, his mind hazed. His eyesight would grow steadily worse as he grew older and he would probably die prematurely. His life would be dependent upon the grace of others; he knew this – he would become this if he lost the runesword's alien aid. But he feared and resented the sword's power – hated it bitterly for the chaos it had wrought in his brain and spirit. In an agony of uncertainty he held the blade in his hands and forced himself to weigh the factors involved. Without the sinister sword, he would lose pride – perhaps even life – but he might know the soothing tranquillity of pure rest; with it he would have power and strength – but the sword would guide him on to evil paths and into a doom-racked future. He would savour power – but never peace. Never calm, sad peacefulness.

He drew a great, sobbing breath and, blind misgiving influencing him, threw the sword into the moondrenched sea.

Incredibly, it did not sink. It did not even float on the water. It fell point forwards into the sea and *stuck* there, quivering as if it were embedded in timber. It remained throbbing in the water, six inches of its blade immersed, and began to give off a weird devil-scream – a howl of horrible malevolence.

With a choking curse erupting from his throat, Elric stretched out his slim, whitely gleaming hand, trying to recover the sentient hellblade. He stretched farther, leaning far out over the rail. He could not grasp it – it lay some feet from him, still. Gasping, a sickening sense of defeat overwhelming him, he dropped over the side and plunged into the bone-chilling water, striking out with strained, grotesque strokes, towards the hovering sword. He was beaten – the sword had won.

He reached it and put his fingers around the hilt. At once it settled in his hand and Elric felt strength seep slowly back into his aching body. Then he realised that he and the sword were interdependent, for though he needed the blade, *Stormbringer*, parasitic, required a user – without a man to wield it, the blade was also powerless.

'We must be bound to one another then,' Elric murmured despairingly. 'Bound by hell-forged chains and fate-haunted circumstance. Well, then – let it be thus so – and men will have cause to tremble, and flee when they hear the names of Elric of Melniboné and *Stormbringer*, his sword. We are two of a kind – produced by an age which has deserted us. Let us give this age *cause* to hate us as we wander its young lands and new-formed seas!'

Strong again, Elric sheathed *Stormbringer* and the sword settled against his side; then, with powerful strokes, he began to swim towards the island while the men he left on the ship breathed with relief and speculated whether he would live or perish in the bleak waters of that strange and nameless sea ...

While the Gods Laugh

1

ONE NIGHT, as Elric sat moodily drinking alone in a tavern, a wingless woman of Myyrrhn came gliding out of the storm and rested her lithe body against him.

Her face was thin and frail-boned, almost as white as Elric's own albino skin, and she wore flimsy pale-green robes which contrasted well with her dark red hair.

The tavern was ablaze with candle-flame and alive with droning argument and gusty laughter, but the words of the woman of Myyrrhn came clear and liquid, carrying over the zesty din.

'I have sought you twenty days,' she said to Elric who regarded her insolently through hooded crimson eyes and lazed in a high-backed chair; a silver wine-cup in his long-fingered right hand and his left on the pommel of his sorcerous rune-sword *Stormbringer*.

'Twenty days,' murmured the Melnibonéan softly, speaking as if to himself; deliberately rude. 'A long time for a beautiful and lonely woman to be wandering the world.' He opened his eyes a trifle wider and spoke to her directly: 'I am Elric of Melniboné, as you evidently know. I grant no favours and ask none. Bearing this in mind, tell me why you have sought me for twenty days.'

Equably, the woman replied, undaunted by the albino's supercilious tone. 'You are a bitter man, Elric; I know this also – and you are grief-haunted for reasons which are already legend. I ask you no favours – but bring you myself and a proposition. What do you desire most in the world?'

'Peace,' Elric told her simply. Then he smiled ironically and said: 'I am an evil man, lady, and my destiny is hell-doomed, but I am not unwise, nor unfair. Let me remind you a little of the truth. Call this legend if you prefer – I do not care.

'A woman died a year ago, on the blade of my trusty sword.'

40

He patted the blade sharply and his eyes were suddenly hard and self-mocking. 'Since then I have courted no woman and desired none. Why should I break such secure habits? If asked, I grant you that I could speak poetry to you, and that you have a grace and beauty which moves me to interesting speculation, but I would not load any part of my dark burden upon one as exquisite as you. Any relationship between us, other than formal, would necessitate my unwilling shifting of part of that burden.' He paused for an instant and then said slowly: 'I should admit that I scream in my sleep sometimes and am often tortured by incommunicable self-loathing. Go while you can, lady, and forget Elric for he can bring only grief to your soul.'

With a quick movement he turned his gaze from her and lifted the silver wine-cup, draining it and replenishing it from a jug at his side.

'No,' said the wingless woman of Myrrhn calmly, 'I will not. Come with me.'

She rose and gently took Elric's hand. Without knowing why, Elric allowed himself to be led from the tavern and out into the wild, rainless storm which howled around the Filkharian city of Raschil. A protective and cynical smile hovered about his mouth as she drew him towards the sea-lashed quayside where she told him her name. Shaarilla of the Dancing Mist, wingless daughter of a dead necromancer – a cripple in her own strange land, and an outcast.

Elric felt uncomfortably drawn to this calm-eyed woman who wasted few words. He felt a great surge of emotion well within him; emotion he had never thought to experience again, and he wanted to take her finely moulded shoulders and press her slim body to his. But he quelled the urge and studied her marble delicacy and her wild hair which flowed in the wind about her head.

Silence rested comfortably between them while the chaotic wind howled mournfully over the sea. Here, Elric could ignore the warm stink of the city and he felt almost relaxed. At last, looking away from him towards the swirling sea, her green robe curling in the wind, she said: 'You have heard, of course, of the Dead Gods' Book?'

Elric nodded. He was interested, despite the need he felt to disassociate himself as much as possible from his fellows. The mythical book was believed to contain knowledge which could solve many problems that had plagued men for centuries – it held a holy and mighty wisdom which every sorcerer desired to sample. But it was believed destroyed, hurled into the sun when the Old Gods were dying in the cosmic wastes which lay beyond the outer reaches of the solar system. Another legend, apparently of later origin, spoke vaguely of the dark ones who had interrupted the Book's sunward coursing and had stolen it before it could be destroyed. Most scholars discounted this legend, arguing that, by this time, the book would have come to light if it did still exist.

Elric made himself speak flatly so that he appeared to be disinterested when he answered Shaarilla. 'Why do you mention the Book?'

'I know that it exists,' Shaarilla replied intensely, 'and I know where it is. My father acquired the knowledge just before he died. Myself – and the book – you may have if you will help me get it.'

Could the secret of peace be contained in the book? Elric wondered. Would he, if he found it, be able to dispense with his hated runesword, *Stormbringer*?

'If you want it so badly that you seek my help,' he said eventually, 'why do you not wish to keep it?'

'Because I would be afraid to have such a thing perpetually in my custody – it is not a book for a woman to own, but you are possibly the last mighty nigromancer left in the world and it is fitting that you should have it. Besides, you might kill me to obtain it – I would never be safe with such a volume in my hands. I need only one small part of its wisdom.'

'What is that?' Elric inquired, studying her patrician beauty with a new pulse stirring within him.

Her mouth set and the lids fell over her eyes. 'When we have the book in our hands – then you will have your answer. Not before.'

'This answer is good enough,' Elric remarked quickly, seeing that he would gain no more information at that stage. 'And the answer appeals to me.' Then, half before he realised it, he seized her shoulders in his slim, pale hands and pressed his colourless lips to her scarlet mouth.

Book, Elric? What do you believe you will find in it?'

Elric shrugged, dismissing the question, but she repeated her words less slowly, with more insistence.

'Very well then,' he said eventually. 'But it is not easy to answer you in a few sentences. I desire, if you like, to know one of two things.'

'And what is that, Elric?'

The tall albino dropped the folded tent to the grass and sighed. His fingers played nervously with the pommel of his runesword. 'Does an ultimate God exist – or not? That is what I need to know, Shaarilla, if my life is to have any direction at all.

'Does Law or Chaos govern our lives? Men need a God, so the philosophers tell us. Have they made one – or did one make them? We know that the Old Gods, as we call them, once lived and are now dead. But were they superior beings to us, or simply like men only wiser? They were not, as far as we know, *ultimate* beings, for they are dead.'

Shaarilla put a hand on Elric's arm. 'Why must you know?' she said.

'Despairingly, sometimes, I seek the comfort of a God, Shaarilla. My mind goes out, lying awake at night, searching through the black barrenness of space for something – anything – which will take me to it, warm me, protect me, tell me that there is order in the chaotic tumble of the universe; that it is consistent, this precision of the planets, not simply a brief, bright spark of sanity in an eternity of malevolent anarchy.'

Elric sighed and his quiet tones were tinged with hopelessness. 'Without a God, a sensitivity to the order of things – of climbing destiny – without this, my only comfort is to attempt, equably, to accept the anarchy. This way, I can revel in chaos and know, without fear, that we are all doomed from the start – that our creeping flash through time is meaningless and damned. I can accept, then, that we are more than forsaken, because there was never anything there to forsake us. Sometimes this is comforting to know – sometimes it is mind-shattering and I gape at myself in horror, wondering why I should believe in anarchy and evil when so much proof exists to the contrary. I have weighed the proof, Shaarilla, and believe that anarchy prevails, in spite of all the laws which seemingly govern our

45

actions, our sorcery, our logic. I see only chaos in the world. If the Book we seek tells me otherwise, then I shall gladly believe it. Until then, I will put my trust only in my sword and myself.'

Shaarilla stared at Elric strangely. 'Not all your words inspire me with feeling,' she said, 'but I believe I know what you mean. Could not this philosophy of yours have been influenced by recent events in your past, however? Do you, perhaps, fear the consequences of your murder and treachery? Is it not more comforting for you to believe in anarchy and deserts which are rarely just?'

Elric turned on her, crimson eyes blazing in anger, but even as he made to speak, the anger fled him and he dropped his eyes towards the ground, hooding them from her gaze.

'Perhaps,' he said lamely. 'I do not know. That is the only *real* truth, Shaarilla. *I do not know.*'

Shaarilla nodded understandingly, her face lit by an enigmatic sympathy; but Elric did not see the look she gave him, for his own eyes were full of crystal tears which flowed down his lean, white face and took his strength and will momentarily from him.

'I am a man possessed,' he groaned, 'and without this devil-blade I carry – I would not be a man at all.'

2

They mounted their swift black horses and spurred them with abandoned savagery down the hillside towards the Marsh, their cloaks whipping behind them as the wind caught them, lashing them high into the air. Both rode with set, hard faces, refusing to acknowledge the aching uncertainty which lurked within them.

And the horses' hooves had splashed into quaking bogland before they could halt.

Cursing, Elric tugged hard on his reins, pulling his horse back on to firm ground. Shaarilla, too, fought her own panicky stallion and guided the beast to the safety of the turf.

'How do we cross?' Elric asked her impatiently.

'There was a map – ' Shaarilla began hesitantly.

'*Where is it?*'

'It – it was lost. I lost it. But I tried hard to memorise it. I

46

think I'll be able to get us safely across.'

'How did you lose it – and why didn't you tell me of this before?' Elric stormed.

'I'm sorry, Elric – but for a whole day, just before I found you in that tavern, my memory was gone. Somehow, I lived through a day without knowing it – and when I awoke, the map was missing.'

Elric frowned. 'There is some force working against us, I am sure,' he muttered, 'but what it is, I do not know.' He raised his voice and said to her: 'Let us hope that your memory is not too faulty, now. These Marshes are infamous the world over, but by all accounts, only natural hazards wait for us.' He grimaced and put his fingers around the hilt of his rune-sword. 'Best go first, Shaarilla, but stay close. Lead the way.'

She nodded, dumbly, and turned her horse's head towards the north, galloping along the bank until she came to a place where a great, tapering rock loomed. Here, a grassy path, four feet or so across, led out into the misty marsh. They could only see a little distance ahead, because of the clinging mist, but it seemed that the trail remained firm for some way. Shaarilla walked her horse on to the path and jolted forward at a slow trot, Elric following immediately behind her.

Through the swirling, heavy mist which shone whitely, the horses moved hesitantly and their riders had to keep them on short, tight rein. The mist padded the marsh with silence and the gleaming, watery fens around them stank with foul putrescence. No animal scurried, no bird shrieked above them. Everywhere was a haunting, fear-laden silence which made both horses and riders uneasy.

With panic in their throats, Elric and Shaarilla rode on, deeper and deeper into the unnatural Marshes of the Mist, their eyes wary and even their nostrils quivering for scent of danger in the stinking morass.

Hours later, when the sun was long past its zenith, Shaarilla's horse reared, screaming and whinnying. She shouted for Elric, her exquisite features twisted in fear as she stared into the mist. He spurred his own bucking horse forwards and joined her.

Something moved, slowly, menacingly in the clinging whiteness. Elric's right hand whipped over to his left side and grasped the hilt of *Stormbringer*.

47

The blade shrieked out of its scabbard, a black fire gleaming along its length and alien power flowing from it into Elric's arm and through his body. A weird, unholy light leapt into Elric's crimson eyes and his mouth was wrenched into a hideous grin as he forced the frightened horse farther into the skulking mist.

'Arioch, Lord of the Seven Darknesses, be with me now!' Elric yelled as he made out the shifting shape ahead of him. It was white, like the mist, yet somehow *darker*. It stretched high above Elric's head. It was nearly eight feet tall and almost as broad. But it was still only an outline, seeming to have no face or limbs – only movement: darting, malevolent movement!

Elric could feel his horse's great heart beating between his legs as the beast plunged forward under its rider's iron control. Shaarilla was screaming something behind him, but he could not hear the words. Elric hacked at the white shape, but his sword met only mist and it howled angrily. The fear-crazed horse would go no farther and Elric was forced to dismount.

'Keep hold of the steed,' he shouted behind him to Shaarilla and moved on light feet towards the darting shape which hovered ahead of him, blocking his path.

Now he could make out some of its saliencies. Two eyes, the colour of thin, yellow wine, were set high in the thing's body, though it had no separate head. A mouthing, obscene slit, filled with fangs, lay just beneath the eyes. It had no nose or ears that Elric could see. Four appendages sprang from its upper parts and its lower body slithered along the ground, unsupported by any limbs. Elric's eyes ached as he looked at it. It was incredibly disgusting to behold and its amorphous body gave off a stench of death and decay. Fighting down his fear, the albino inched forward warily, his sword held high to parry any thrust the thing might make with its arms. Elric recognised it from a description in one of his grimoires. It was a Mist Giant – possibly the only Mist Giant, Bellbane. Even the wisest wizards were uncertain how many existed – one or many. It was a ghoul of the swamp-lands which fed off the souls and the blood of men and beasts. But the Marshes of this Mist were far to the east of Bellbane's reputed haunts.

Elric ceased to wonder why so few animals inhabited that stretch of the swamp. Overhead the sky was beginning to darken.

Stormbringer throbbed in Elric's gasp as he called the names of the ancient, evil Demon-Gods of his people. The nauseous ghoul obviously recognised the names. For an instant, it wavered backwards. Elric made his legs move towards the thing. Now he saw that the ghoul was not white at all. But it had no colour to it that Elric could recognise. There was a suggestion of orangeness dashed with sickening greenish yellow, but he did not see the colours with his eyes – he only *sensed* the alien, unholy tinctures.

Then Elric rushed towards the thing, shouting the names which now had no meaning to his surface consciousness. '*Balaan – Marthim! Aesma! Alastor! Saebos! Verdelet! Nizilfkm! Haborym!* Haborym of the Fires Which Destroy!' His whole mind was torn in two. Part of him wanted to run, to hide, but he had no control over the power which now gripped him and pushed him to meet the horror. His sword blade hacked and slashed at the shape. It was like trying to cut through water – sentient, pulsating water. But *Stormbringer* had effect. The whole shape of the ghoul quivered as if in dreadful pain. Elric felt himself plucked into the air and his vision went. He could see nothing – do nothing but hack and cut at the thing which now held him.

Sweat poured from him as, blindly, he fought on.

Pain which was hardly physical – a deeper, horrifying pain, filled his being as he howled now in agony and struck continually at the yielding bulk which embraced him and was pulling him slowly towards its gaping maw. He struggled and writhed in the obscene grasp of the thing. With powerful arms, it was holding him, almost lasciviously, drawing him closer as a rough lover would draw a girl. Even the mighty power intrinsic in the runesword did not seem enough to kill the monster. Though its efforts were somewhat weaker than earlier, it still drew Elric nearer to the gnashing, slavering mouth-slit.

Elric cried out the names of his Gods again, while *Stormbringer* danced and sang an evil song in his right hand. In agony, Elric writhed, praying, begging and promising, but still he was drawn inch by inch towards the grinning maw.

Savagely, grimly, he fought and a dreadful name formed deep in his throat and forced itself through protesting vocal chords until it seethed piercingly from the albino's contracted mouth. It was the ultimate name – incredibly evil in its soul-shaking implications. Almost imperceptibly, the Mist Giant weakened. Feeling that he was, at last, beginning to make a definite impression on the Giant's dreadful dynamism though his mind and limbs were shuddering, Elric pressed his advantage and the knowledge that the ghoul was losing its strength gave him more power. Blindly, the agony piercing every nerve of his body, he struck and struck.

Then, quite suddenly, he was falling.

He seemed to fall for hours, slowly, weightlessly until he landed upon a surface which yielded beneath him. He began to sink.

Far off, beyond time and space, he heard a distant voice calling to him. He did not want to hear it; he was content to lie where he was as the cold, comforting stuff in which he lay dragged him slowly into itself.

Then some sixth sense made him realise that it was Shaarilla's voice calling him and he forced himself to make sense out of her words.

'*Elric – the marsh! You're in the marsh. Don't move!*'

He smiled to himself. Why should he move? Down he was sinking, slowly, calmly – down into the welcoming marsh . . .

With a mental jolt, full awareness of the situation came back to him and he jerked his eyes open. Above him was mist. To one side a pool of unnamable colouring was slowly evaporating, giving off a foul odour. On the other side he could just make out a human form, gesticulating wildly. Beyond the human form were the barely discernible shapes of two horses. Shaarilla was there. Beneath him –

Beneath him was the marsh.

Thick, stinking slime was sucking him downwards as he lay spread-eagled upon it, half-submerged already. *Stormbringer* was still in his right hand. He could just see it if he turned his head. Carefully, he tried to lift the top half of his body from the sucking morass. He succeeded, only to feel his legs sink deeper. Sitting upright, he shouted to the girl.

'Shaarilla! Quickly – a rope!'

'There is no rope, Elric!' She was ripping off her top garment, frantically tearing it into strips.

50

Still Elric sank, his feet finding no purchase beneath them.

Shaarilla hastily knotted the strips of cloth. She flung the makeshift rope inexpertly towards the sinking albino. It fell short. Fumbling in her haste, she threw it again. This time his groping left hand found it. The girl began to haul on the fabric. Elric felt himself rise a little and then stop.

'It's no good, Elric – I haven't the strength.'

Cursing her, Elric shouted: 'The horse – tie your end to the horse!'

She ran towards one of the horses and looped the cloth around the pommel of the saddle. Then she tugged at the beast's reins and began to walk it away.

Swiftly, Elric was dragged from the sucking bog and, still gripping *Stormbringer* was pulled to the inadequate safety of the strip of turf.

Gasping, he tried to stand, but found his legs incredibly weak beneath him. He rose, staggered, and fell. Shaarilla knelt down beside him.

'Are you hurt?'

Elric smiled in spite of his weakness. 'I don't think so.'

'It was dreadful. I couldn't see properly what was happening. You seemed to disappear and then – then you screamed that – that *word*.' She was trembling, her face pale and taut.

'What word?' Elric was genuinely puzzled. 'What word did I scream?'

She shook her head. 'It doesn't matter – but whatever it was – it saved you. You reappeared soon afterwards and fell into the marsh . . . '

Stormbringer's power was still flowing into the albino. He already felt stronger.

With an effort, he got up and stumbled unsteadily towards his horse.

'I'm sure that the Mist Giant does not usually haunt this marsh – it was sent here. By what – or whom – I don't know, but we must get to firmer ground while we can.'

Shaarilla said: 'Which way – back or forward?'

Elric frowned. 'Why, forward, of course. Why do you ask?'

She swallowed and shook her head. 'Let's hurry, then,' she said.

They mounted their horses and rode with little caution until

51

the marsh and its cloak of mist was behind them.

Now the journey took on a new urgency as Elric realised that some force was attempting to put obstacles in their way. They rested little and savagely rode their powerful horses to a virtual standstill.

On the fifth day they were riding through barren, rocky country and light rain was falling.

The hard ground was slippery so that they were forced to ride more slowly, huddled over the sodden necks of their horses, muffled in cloaks which only inadequately kept out the drizzling rain. They had ridden in silence for some time before they heard a ghastly cackling baying ahead of them and the rattle of hooves.

Elric motioned towards a large rock looming to their right. 'Shelter there,' he said. 'Something comes towards us – possibly more enemies. With luck, they'll pass us.' Shaarilla mutely obeyed him and together they waited as the hideous baying grew nearer.

'One rider – several other beasts,' Elric said, listening intently. 'The beasts either follow or pursue the rider.'

Then they were in sight – racing through the rain. A man frantically spurring an equally frightened horse – and behind him, the distance decreasing, a pack of what at first appeared to be dogs. But these were not dogs – they were half-dog and half-bird, with the lean, shaggy bodies and legs of dogs but possessing birdlike talons in place of paws and savagely curved beaks which snapped where muzzles should have been.

'The hunting dogs of the Dharzi!' gasped Shaarilla. 'I thought that they, like their masters, were long extinct!'

'I, also,' Elric said. 'What are they doing in these parts? There was never contact between the Dharzi and the dwellers of this Land?'

'Brought here – by *something*,' Shaarilla whispered. 'Those devil-dogs will scent us to be sure.'

Elric reached for his runesword. 'Then we can lose nothing by aiding their quarry,' he said, urging his mount forward. 'Wait here, Shaarilla.'

By this time, the devil-pack and the man they pursued were rushing past the sheltering rock, speeding down a narrow defile. Elric spurred his horse down the slope.

'Ho there!' he shouted to the frantic rider. 'Turn and stand,

52

my friend – I'm here to aid you!'

His moaning runesword lifted high, Elric thundered towards the snapping, howling devil-dogs and his horse's hooves struck one with an impact which broke the unnatural beast's spine. There were some five or six of the weird dogs left. The rider turned his horse and drew a long sabre from a scabbard at his waist. He was a small man, with a broad ugly mouth. He grinned in relief.

'A lucky chance, this meeting, good master!'

This was all he had time to remark before two of the dogs were leaping at him and he was forced to give his whole attention to defending himself from their slashing talons and snapping beaks.

The other three dogs concentrated their vicious attention upon Elric. One leapt high, its beak aimed at Elric's throat. He felt foul breath on his face and hastily brought *Stormbringer* round in an arc which chopped the dog in two. Filthy blood spattered Elric and his horse and the scent of it seemed to increase the fury of the other dogs' attack. But the blood made the dancing black runesword sing an almost ecstatic tune and Elric felt it writhe in his grasp and stab at another of the hideous dogs. The point caught the beast just below its breastbone as it reared up at the albino. It screamed in terrible agony and turned its beak to seize the blade. As the beak connected with the lambent black metal of the sword, a foul stench, akin to the smell of burning, struck Elric's nostrils and the beast's scream broke off sharply.

Engaged with the remaining devil-dog, Elric caught a fleeting glimpse of the charred corpse. His horse was rearing high, lashing at the last alien animal with flailing hooves. The dog avoided the horse's attack and came at Elric's unguarded left side. The albino swung in the saddle and brought his sword hurtling down to slice into the dog's skull and spill brains and blood on the wetly gleaming ground. Still somehow alive, the dog snapped feebly at Elric, but the Melnibonéan ignored its futile attack and turned his attention to the little man who had dispensed with one of his adversaries, but was having difficulty with the second. The dog had grasped the sabre with its beak, gripping the sword near the hilt.

Talons raked towards the little man's throat as he strove to shake the dog's grip. Elric charged forward, his runesword aimed like a lance to where the devil-dog dangled in mid-air, its talons slashing, trying to reach the flesh of its former quarry. *Stormbringer* caught the beast in its lower abdomen and ripped upwards, slitting the thing's underparts from crutch to throat. It released its hold on the small man's sabre and fell writhing to the ground. Elric's horse trampled it into the rocky ground. Breathing heavily, the albino sheathed *Stormbringer* and warily regarded the man he had saved. He disliked unnecessary contact with anyone and did not wish to be embarrassed by a display of emotion on the little man's part.

He was not disappointed, for the wide, ugly mouth split into a cheerful grin and the man bowed in the saddle as he returned his own curved blade to its scabbard.

'Thanks, good sir,' he said lightly. 'Without your help, the battle might have lasted longer. You deprived me of good sport, but you meant well. Moonglum is my name.'

'Elric of Melniboné, I,' replied the albino, but saw no reaction on the little man's face. This was strange, for the name of Elric was infamous throughout most of the world. The story of his treachery and the slaying of his cousin Cymoril had been told and elaborated upon in every tavern in the civilised world. Much as he hated it, he was used to receiving some indication of recognition from those he met. His albinism was enough to mark him.

Intrigued by Moonglum's ignorance, and feeling strangely drawn towards the cocky little rider, Elric studied him in an effort to discover from what land he came. Moonglum wore no armour and his clothes were of faded blue material, travel-stained and worn. A stout leather belt carried the sabre, a dirk and a woollen purse. Upon his feet, Moonglum wore ankle-length boots of cracked leather. His horse-furniture was much used but of obviously good quality. The man himself, seated high in the saddle, was barely more than five feet tall, with legs too long, in proportion, to the rest of his slight body. His nose was short and uptilted, beneath grey-green eyes, large and innocent-seeming. A mop of vivid red hair fell over his forehead and down his neck, unrestrained. He sat his horse comfortably, still grinning but looking now behind Elric to where Shaarilla rode to join them.

Moonglum bowed elaborately as the girl pulled her horse to a halt.

Elric said coldly, 'The Lady Shaarilla – Master Moonglum of — ?'

'Of Elwher,' Moonglum supplied. 'The mercantile capital of the East – the finest city in the Young Kingdoms.'

Elric recognised the name. 'So you are from Elwher, Master Moonglum. I have heard of the place. A new city, is it not? Some few centuries old. You have ridden far.'

'Indeed I have, sir. Without knowledge of the language used in these parts, the journey would have been harder, but luckily the slave who inspired me with tales of his homeland taught me the speech thoroughly.'

'But why do you travel these parts – have you not heard the legends?' Shaarilla spoke incredulously.

'Those very legends were what brought me hence – and I'd begun to discount them, until those unpleasant pups set upon me. For what reason they decided to give chase, I will not know, for I gave them no cause to take a dislike to me. This is, indeed, a barbarous land.'

Elric was uncomfortable. Light talk of the kind which Moonglum seemed to enjoy was contrary to his own brooding nature. But in spite of this, he found that he was liking the man more and more.

It was Moonglum who suggested that they travel together for a while. Shaarilla objected, giving Elric a warning glance, but he ignored it.

'Very well then, friend Moonglum, since three are stronger than two, we'd appreciate your company. We ride towards the mountains.' Elric, himself, was feeling in a more cheerful mood.

'And what do you seek there?' Moonglum inquired.

'A secret,' Elric said, and his new-found companion was discreet enough to drop the question.

3

So they rode, while the rainfall increased and splashed and sang among the rocks with the sky like dull steel above them and the wind crooning a dirge about their ears. Three small figures riding swiftly towards the black mountain barrier which rose over the world like a brooding God. And perhaps it was a God that laughed sometimes as they neared the foothills of the range, or perhaps it was the wind whistling through the dark mystery of canyons and precipices and the tumble of basalt and granite which climbed towards lonely peaks. Thunder clouds formed around those peaks and lightning smashed downwards like a monster finger searching the earth for grubs. Thunder rattled over the range and Shaarilla spoke her thoughts at last to Elric; spoke them as the mountains came in sight.

'Elric – let us go back, I beg you. Forget the Book – there are too many forces working against us. Take heed of the signs, Elric, or we are doomed!'

But Elric was grimly silent, for he had long been aware that the girl was losing her enthusiasm for the quest she had started.

'Elric – please. We will never reach the Book. Elric, turn back.'

She rode beside him, pulling at his garments until impatiently he shrugged himself clear of her grasp and said:

'Too late, Shaarilla. I am intrigued too much to stop now. Either continue to lead the way – or tell me what you know and stay here. You desired to sample the Book's wisdom once – but now a few minor pitfalls on our journey have frightened you. What was it you needed to learn, Shaarilla?'

She did not answer him, but said instead: 'And what was it you desired, Elric? Peace, you told me. Well, I warn you, you'll find no peace in those grim mountains – if we reach them at all.'

'You have not been frank with me, Shaarilla,' Elric said coldly, still looking ahead of him at the black peaks. 'You know something of the forces seeking to stop us.'

She shrugged. 'It matters not – I know little. My father spoke a few vague warnings before he died, that is all.'

'What did he say?'

'He said that He who guards the Book would use all his power to stop mankind from using its wisdom.'

'What else?'

'Nothing else, Elric. But it is enough, now that I see that my father's warning was truly spoken. It was this guardian who killed him, Elric – or one of the guardian's minions. I do not

56

wish to suffer that fate, in spite of what the Book might do for me. I had thought you powerful enough to aid me – but now I doubt it.'

'I have protected you so far,' Elric said simply. 'Now tell me what you seek from the Book?'

'I am too ashamed.'

Elric did not press the question, but eventually she spoke softly, almost whispering. 'I sought my wings,' she said.

'Your wings – you mean the Book might give you a spell so that you could grow wings!' Elric smiled ironically 'And that is why you seek the vessel of the world's mightiest wisdom!'

'If you were thought deformed in your own land – it would seem important enough to you,' she shouted defiantly.

Elric turned his face towards her, his crimson-irised eyes burning with a strange emotion. He put a hand to his dead-white skin and a crooked smile twisted his lips. 'I, too, have felt as you do,' he said quietly. That was all he said and Shaarilla dropped behind him again, feeling somehow ashamed and wretched.

They rode on in silence until Moonglum, who had been riding discreetly ahead, cocked his overlarge skull on one side and suddenly drew rein.

Elric joined him. 'What is it, Moonglum?'

'I hear horses coming this way,' the little man said. 'And voices which are disturbingly familiar. More of those devil-dogs, Elric – and this time accompanied by riders!'

Elric, too, heard the sounds, now, and shouted a warning to Shaarilla.

'Perhaps you were right,' he called. 'More trouble comes towards us.'

'What now?' Moonglum said, frowning.

'Ride for the mountains,' Elric replied, 'and we may yet outdistance them.'

They spurred their steeds into a fast gallop and sped towards the hills.

But their flight was hopeless. Soon a black pack was visible on the horizon and the sharp birdlike baying of the devil-dogs drew nearer. Elric stared backward at their pursuers. Night was beginning to fall, and visibility was decreasing with every passing moment but he had a vague impression of the riders who raced behind the pack. They were swathed in dark cloaks and carried long spears. Their faces were invisible, lost in the shadow of the hoods which covered their heads.

Now Elric and his companions were forcing their horses up a steep incline, seeking the shelter of the rocks which lay above.

'We'll halt here,' Elric ordered, 'and try and hold them off. In the open they could easily surround us.'

Moonglum nodded affirmatively, agreeing with the good sense contained in Elric's words. They pulled their sweating steeds to a standstill and prepared to join battle with the howling pack and their dark-cloaked masters.

Soon the first of the devil-dogs were rushing up the incline, their beak-jaws slavering and their talons rattling on stone. Standing between two rocks, blocking the way between with their bodies, Elric and Moonglum met the first attack and quickly dispatched three of the animals. Several more took the place of the dead and the first of the riders was visible behind them as night crept closer.

'Xiros!' swore Elric, suddenly recognising the riders. 'These are the Lords of Dharzi – dead these ten centuries. We're fighting dead men, Moonglum, and the too-tangible ghosts of their dogs. Unless I can think of a sorcerous means to defeat them, we're doomed!'

The zombie-men appeared to have no intention of taking part in the attack for the moment. They waited, their dead eyes eerily luminous, as the devil-dogs attempted to break through the singing network of steel with which Elric and his companion defended themselves. Elric was racking his brains – trying to dredge a spoken spell from his memory which would dismiss these living dead. Then it came to him, and hoping that the forces he had to invoke would decide to aid him, he began to chant:

> 'Let the Laws which govern all things
> Not so lightly be dismissed;
> Let the Ones who flaunt the Earth Kings
> With a fresher death be kissed.'

Nothing happened. 'I've failed.' Elric muttered hopelessly as he met the attack of a snapping devil-dog and spitted the thing on his sword.

But then – the ground rocked and seemed to seethe beneath the feet of the horses upon whose backs the dead men sat. The tremor lasted a few seconds and then subsided.

'The spell was not powerful enough,' Elric sighed.

The earth trembled again and small craters formed in the ground of the hillside upon which the dead Lords of Dharzi impassively waited. Stones crumbled and the horses stamped nervously. Then the earth rumbled.

'Back!' yelled Elric warningly. 'Back – or we'll go with them!' They retreated – backing towards Shaarilla and their waiting horses as the ground sagged beneath their feet. The Dharzi mounts were rearing and snorting and the remaining dogs turned nervously to regard their masters with puzzled, uncertain eyes. A low moan was coming from the lips of the living dead. Suddenly, a whole area of the surrounding hillside split into cracks, and yawning crannies appeared in the surface. Elric and his companions swung themselves on to their horses as, with a frightful multi-voiced scream, the dead Lords were swallowed by the earth, returning to the depths from which they had been summoned.

A deep unholy chuckle arose from the shattered pit. It was the mocking laughter of the Earth Kings taking their rightful prey back into their keeping. Whining, the devil-dogs slunk towards the edge of the pit, sniffing around it. Then, with one accord, the black pack hurled itself down into the chasm, following its masters to whatever cold doom awaited them.

Moonglum shuddered. 'You are on familiar terms with the strangest people, friend Elric,' he said shakily and turned his horse towards the mountains again.

They reached the black mountains on the following day and nervously Shaarilla led them along the rocky route she had memorised. She no longer pleaded with Elric to return – she was resigned to whatever fate awaited them. Elric's obsession was burning within him and he was filled with impatience – certain that he would find, at last, the ultimate truth of existence in the Dead Gods' Book. Moonglum was cheerfully sceptical, while Shaarilla was consumed with foreboding.

Rain still fell and the storm still growled and crackled above them. And, as the driving rainfall increased with fresh insistence,

59

they came, at last, to the black, gaping mouth of a huge cave.

'I can lead you no further,' Shaarilla said wearily. 'The Book lies somewhere beyond the entrance to this cave.'

Elric and Moonglum looked uncertainly at one another, neither of them sure what move to make next. To have reached their goal seemed somehow anticlimatic – for nothing blocked the cave entrance – and nothing appeared to guard it.

'It is inconceivable,' said Elric, 'that the dangers which beset us were not engineered by something, yet here we are – and no one seeks to stop us entering. Are you sure that this is the *right* cave, Shaarilla?'

The girl pointed upwards to the rock above the entrance. Engraved in it was a curious symbol which Elric instantly recognised.

'The sign of Chaos!' Elric exclaimed. 'Perhaps I should have guessed in what we have become caught up!'

'What does it mean, Elric?' Moonglum asked.

'That is the symbol of everlasting disruption and anarchy,' Elric told him. 'We are standing in territory presided over by the Lords of Entropy or one of their minions. So that is who our enemy is! This can only mean one thing – the Book is of extreme importance to the order of things on this planet – possibly the galaxy – or the entire universe!'

Moonglum stared at him in puzzlement. The two latter terms meant nothing to him. 'What do you mean, Elric?'

'It is believed by many sorcerers and philosophers that two forces govern the universe – fighting an eternal battle,' Elric replied. 'These two forces are termed Law and Chaos. These are values supposedly set above the qualities men call Good and Evil. The upholders of Chaos state that in such a world as they rule, all things are possible. Opponents of Chaos – those who ally themselves with the forces of Law – say that without Law *nothing* material is possible.

'I, like most sorcerers, stand apart, believing that a balance between the two is the proper state of things. However, I can see now that we have become embroiled in a dispute between the two forces. The Book is valuable to either faction, obviously, and I could guess that the minions of Entropy are worried what power we might release if we obtain this Book. They are supposed to be governed by some Code which prohibits them from interfering directly in men's lives – that is why we have not been aware of their presence. Now perhaps, I will discover at last the answer to the one question which concerns me – does an ultimate force rule over the opposing factions of Law and Chaos?'

Elric stepped through the cave entrance, peering into the gloom while the others hesitantly followed him.

'The cave stretches back a long way. All we can do is press on until we find its far wall,' Elric said.

'Let's hope that its far wall lies not *downwards*,' Moonglum said ironically as he motioned Elric to lead on.

They stumbled forward as the cave grew darker and darker. Their voices were magnified and hollow to their own ears as the floor of the cave slanted sharply down.

'This is no cave,' Elric whispered, 'it's a *tunnel* – but I cannot guess where it leads.'

For several hours they pressed onwards in pitch darkness, clinging to one another as they reeled forward, uncertain of their footing and still aware that they were moving down a gradual incline. They lost all sense of time and Elric began to feel as if he were living through a dream. Events seemed to have become so unpredictable and beyond his control that he could no longer cope with thinking about them in ordinary terms. The tunnel was long and dark and wide and cold. It offered no comfort and the floor eventually became the only thing which had any reality. It was firm beneath his feet. He began to feel that possibly he was not moving – that the floor, after all, was moving and he was remaining stationary. His companions clung to him but he was not aware of them. He was lost and his brain was numb. Sometimes he swayed and felt he was on the edge of a precipice. Sometimes he fell and his groaning body met hard stone, disproving the proximity of the gulf down which he half-expected to fall.

All the while he made his legs perform walking motions, even though he was not at all sure whether he was actually moving forward. And time meant nothing – became a meaningless concept with relation to nothing.

Until, at last, he was aware of a faint, blue glow ahead of him and he knew that he had been moving forward. He began to run down the incline, but found that he was going too fast and had to check his speed. There was a scent of alien strangeness in the cool air of the cave tunnel and fear was a fluid force which surged over him, something separate from himself.

The others obviously felt it, too, for though they said nothing, Elric could sense it. Slowly they moved downward, drawn like automatons towards the pale blue glow below them.

And then they were out of the tunnel, staring awestruck at the unearthly vision which confronted them. Above them, the very air seemed of the strange blue colour which had originally attracted them. They were standing on a jutting slab of rock and, although it was still somehow *dark*, the eerie blue glow illuminated a stretch of glinting silver beach beneath them. And the beach was lapped by a surging dark sea which moved restlessly like a liquid giant in disturbed slumber. Scattered along the silver beach were the dim shapes of wrecks – the bones of peculiarly designed boats, each of a different pattern from the rest. The sea surged away into darkness and there was no horizon – only blackness. Behind them, they could see a sheer cliff which was also lost in darkness beyond a certain point. And it was cold – bitterly cold, with an unbelievable sharpness. For though the sea threshed beneath them, there was no dampness in the air – no smell of salt. It was a bleak and awesome sight and, apart from the sea, they were the only things that moved – the only things to make sound, for the sea was horribly silent in its restless movement.

'What now, Elric?' whispered Moonglum, shivering.

Elric shook his head and they continued to stand there for a long time until the albino, his white face and hands ghastly in the alien light, said: 'Since it is impracticable to return – we shall venture over the sea.'

His voice was hollow and he spoke as one who was unaware of his words.

Steps cut into the living rock led down towards the beach and now Elric began to descend them. The others allowed him to lead them staring around them, their eyes lit by a terrible fascination.

4

Their feet profaned the silence as they reached the silver beach of crystalline stones and crunched across it. Elric's crimson eyes fixed upon one of the objects littering the beach and he smiled. He shook his head savagely from side to side, as if to clear it. Trembling, he pointed to one of the boats, and the pair saw that it was intact, unlike the others. It was yellow and red – vulgarly gay in this environment and nearing it they observed that it was made of wood, yet unlike any wood they had seen. Moonglum ran his stubby fingers along its length.

'Hard as iron,' he breathed. 'No wonder it has not rotted as the others have.' He peered inside and shuddered. 'Well the owner won't argue if we take it,' he said wryly.

Elric and Shaarilla understood him when they saw the unnaturally twisted skeleton which lay at the bottom of the boat. Elric reached inside and pulled the thing out, hurling it on to the stones. It rattled and rolled over the gleaming shingle, disintegrating as it did so, scattering bones over a wide area. The skull came to rest by the edge of the beach, seeming to stare sightlessly out over the disturbing ocean.

As Elric and Moonglum strove to push and pull the boat down the beach towards the sea, Shaarilla moved ahead of them and squatted down, putting her hand into the wetness. She stood up sharply, shaking the stuff from her hand.

'This is not water as I know it,' she said. They heard her, but said nothing.

'We'll need a sail,' Elric murmured. The cold breeze was moving out over the ocean. 'A cloak should serve.' He stripped off his cloak and knotted it to the mast of the vessel. 'Two of us will have to hold this at either edge,' he said. 'That way we'll have some slight control over the direction the boat takes. It's makeshift – but the best we can manage.'

They shoved off, taking care not to get their feet in the sea.

The wind caught the sail and pushed the boat out over the ocean, moving at a faster pace than Elric had at first reckoned. The boat began to hurtle forward as if possessed of its own volition and Elric's and Moonglum's muscles ached as they clung to the bottom ends of the sail.

Soon the silver beach was out of sight and they could see little – the pale blue light above them scarcely penetrating the blackness. It was then that they heard the dry flap of wings over their heads and looked up.

Silently descending were three massive ape-like creatures, borne on great leathery wings. Shaarilla recognised them and gasped.

'Clakars!'

Moonglum shrugged as he hurriedly drew his sword – 'A name only – what are they?' But he received no answer for the leading winged ape descended with a rush, mouthing and gibbering, showing long fangs in a slavering snout. Moonglum dropped his portion of the sail and slashed at the beast but it veered away, its huge wings beating, and sailed upwards again.

Elric unsheathed *Stormbringer* – and was astounded. The blade remained silent, its familiar howl of glee muted. The blade shuddered in his hand and instead of the rush of power which usually flowed up his arm, he felt only a slight tingling. He was panic-stricken for a moment – without the sword, he would soon lose all vitality. Grimly fighting down his fear, he used the sword to protect himself from the rushing attack of one of the winged apes.

The ape gripped the blade, bowling Elric over, but it yelled in pain as the blade cut through one knotted hand, severing fingers which lay twitching and bloody on the narrow deck. Elric gripped the side of the boat and hauled himself upright once more. Shrilling its agony, the winged ape attacked again, but this time with more caution. Elric summoned all his strength and swung the heavy sword in a two-handed grip, ripping off one of the leathery wings so that the mutilated beast flopped about the deck. Judging the place where its heart should be, Elric drove the blade in under the breast-bone. The ape's movements subsided.

Moonglum was lashing wildly at two of the winged apes which were attacking him from both sides. He was down on one knee, vainly hacking at random. He had opened up the whole side of a beast's head but, though in pain, it still came at him. Elric hurled *Stormbringer* through the darkness and it struck the wounded beast in the throat, point first. The ape clutched with clawing fingers at the steel and fell overboard. Its corpse floated on the liquid but slowly began to sink. Elric grabbed with frantic fingers at the hilt of his sword, reaching far over the side of the boat. Incredibly, the blade was sinking with the beast. Knowing *Stormbringer*'s properties as he did, Elric was amazed – once when he had hurled the runesword into the ocean, it had refused to sink. Now it was being dragged beneath the surface as any ordinary blade would be dragged. He gripped the hilt and hauled the sword out of the winged ape's carcass.

His strength was seeping swiftly from him. It was incredible. What alien laws governed this cavern world? He could not guess – and all he was concerned with was regaining his waning strength. Without the runesword's power, this was impossible!

Moonglum's curved blade had disembowelled the remaining beast and the little man was busily tossing the dead thing over the side. He turned, grinning triumphantly, to Elric.

'A good fight,' he said.

Elric shook his head. 'We must cross this sea speedily,' he replied, 'else we're lost – finished. My power is gone.'

'How? Why?'

'I know not – unless the forces of Entropy rule more strongly here. Make haste – there is no time for speculation.'

Moonglum's eyes were disturbed. He could do nothing but act as Elric said.

Elric was trembling in his weakness, holding the billowing sail with draining strength. Shaarilla moved to help him, her thin hands close to his; her deep-set eyes bright with sympathy.

'What *were* those things?' Moonglum gasped, his teeth naked and white beneath his back-drawn lips, his breath coming short.

'Clakars,' Shaarilla replied. 'They are the primeval ancestors of my people, older in origin than recorded time. My people are thought the oldest inhabitants of this planet.'

'Whoever seeks to stop us in this quest of yours had best find some – original means.' Moonglum grinned. 'The old methods don't work.' But the other two did not smile, for Elric was half-fainting and the woman was concerned only with his plight. Moonglum shrugged, staring ahead.

When he spoke again, sometime later, his voice was excited. 'We're nearing land!'

Land it was, and they were travelling fast towards it. Too fast. Elric heaved himself upright and spoke heavily and with difficulty. 'Drop the sail!' Moonglum obeyed him. The boat sped on, struck another stretch of silver beach and ground up it, the prow ploughing a dark scar through the glinting shingle. It stopped suddenly, tilting violently to one side so that the three were tumbled against the boat's rail.

Shaarilla and Moonglum pulled themselves upright and dragged the limp and nerveless albino on to the beach. Carrying him between them, they struggled up the beach until the crystalline shingle gave way to thick, fluffy moss, padding their footfalls. They laid the albino down and stared at him worriedly, uncertain of their next actions.

Elric strained to rise, but was unable to do so. 'Give me time,' he gasped. 'I won't die – but already my eyesight is fading. I can only hope that the blade's power will return on dry land.'

With a mighty effort, he pulled *Stormbringer* from its scabbard and he smiled in relief as the evil runesword moaned faintly and then, slowly, its song increased in power as black flame flickered along its length. Already the power was flowing into Elric's body, giving him renewed vitality. But even as strength returned, Elric's crimson eyes flared with terrible misery.

'Without this black blade,' he groaned, 'I am nothing, as you see. But what is it making of me? Am I to be bound to it for ever?'

The others did not answer him and they were both moved by an emotion they could not define – an emotion blended of fear, hate and pity – linked with something else . . .

Eventually, Elric rose, trembling, and silently led them up the mossy hillside towards a more natural light which filtered from above. They could see that it came from a wide chimney, leading apparently to the upper air. By means of the light, they could soon make out a dark, irregular shape which towered in the shadow of the gap.

As they neared the shape, they saw that it was a castle of black stone – a sprawling pile covered with dark green crawling lichen which curled over its ancient bulk with an almost sentient protectiveness. Towers appeared to spring at random from it and it covered a vast area. There seemed to be no windows in any part of it and the only orifice was a rearing doorway blocked by thick bars, of a metal which glowed with dull redness, but without heat. Above this gate, in flaring amber, was the sign of the Lords of Entropy, representing eight arrows radiating from a central hub in all directions. It appeared to hang in the air without touching the black, lichen-covered stone.

'I think our quest ends here,' Elric said grimly. 'Here, or nowhere.'

'Before I go farther, Elric, I'd like to know what it is you seek,' Moonglum murmured. 'I think I've earned the right.'

'A book,' Elric said carelessly. 'The Dead Gods' Book. It lies within those castle walls – of that I'm certain. We have reached the end of our journey.'

Moonglum shrugged. 'I might not have asked,' he smiled, 'for all your words mean to me. I hope that I will be allowed some small share of whatever treasure it represents.'

Elric grinned, in spite of the coldness which gripped his bowels, but he did not answer Moonglum.

'We need to enter the castle, first,' he said instead.

As if the gates had heard him, the metal bars flared to a pale green and then their glow faded back to red and finally dulled into non-existence. The entrance was unbarred and their way apparently clear.

'I like not *that*,' growled Moonglum. 'Too easy. A trap awaits us – are we to spring it at the pleasure of whoever dwells within the castle confines?'

'What else can we do?' Elric spoke quietly.

'Go back – or forward. Avoid the castle – do not tempt He who guards the Book!' Shaarilla was gripping the albino's right arm, her whole face moving with fear, her eyes pleading. 'Forget the Book, Elric!'

'*Now?*' Elric laughed humourlessly. 'Now – after this journey? No, Shaarilla, not when the truth is so close. Better to die than never to have tried to secure the wisdom in the Book when it lies so near.'

Shaarilla's clutching fingers relaxed their grip and her shoulders slumped in hopelessness. 'We cannot do battle with the minions of Entropy . . . '

'Perhaps we will not have to.' Elric did not believe his own words but his mouth was twisted with some dark emotion, intense and terrible. Moonglum glanced at Shaarilla.

'Shaarilla is right,' he said with conviction. 'You'll find nothing but bitterness, possibly death, inside those castle walls. Let us, instead, climb yonder steps and attempt to reach the surface.' He pointed to some twisting steps which led towards the yawning rent in the cavern roof.

Elric shook his head. 'No. You go if you like.'

Moonglum grimaced in perplexity. 'You're a stubborn one, friend Elric. Well, if it's all or nothing – then I'm with you. But personally, I have always preferred compromise.'

Elric began to walk slowly forward towards the dark entrance of the bleak and towering castle.

In a wide, shadowy courtyard a tall figure, wreathed in scarlet fire, stood awaiting them.

Elric marched on, passing through the gateway. Moonglum and Shaarilla nervously followed.

Gusty laughter roared from the mouth of the giant and the scarlet fire fluttered about him. He was naked and unarmed, but the power which flowed from him almost forced the three back. His skin was scaly and of smoky purple colouring. His massive body was alive with rippling muscle as he rested lightly on the balls of his feet. His skull was long, slanting sharply backwards at the forehead and his eyes were like slivers of blue steel, showing no pupil. His whole body shook with mighty, malicious joy.

'*Greetings to you, Lord Elric of Melniboné – I congratulate you for your remarkable tenacity!*'

'Who are you?' Elric growled, his hand on his sword.

'*My name is Orunlu the Keeper and this is a stronghold of the Lords of Entropy.*' The giant smiled cynically. '*You pride yourself on your control over a few nature spirits – you need not finger your puny blade so nervously, for you should know that I cannot harm you now.*'

'So it is true – the minions of Law and Chaos have no power over Men?' Elric's voice betrayed his mounting excitement. 'You cannot stop us?'

'*I do not dare to – since my oblique efforts have failed. But your foolish endeavours perplex me somewhat, I'll admit. The Book is of importance to us – but what can it mean to you? I have guarded it for three hundred centuries and have never been*

68

curious enough to seek to discover why my Masters place so much importance upon it – why they bothered to rescue it on its sunward course and incarcerate it on this boring ball of earth populated by the capering, briefly-lived clowns you call men?'

'I seek in it the Truth,' Elric said guardedly, feeling foolish.

'There is no Truth but that of Eternal struggle,' the scarlet-flamed giant said with conviction.

'What rules above the forces of Law and Chaos?' Elric asked. 'What controls your destinies as it controls mine?'

The giant frowned.

'That question, I cannot answer. I do not know.'

'Then perhaps the Book will tell us both,' Elric said purposefully. 'Let me pass – tell me where it lies.'

The giant moved back, smiling ironically. *'It lies in a small chamber in the central tower. I have sworn never to venture there, otherwise I might even lead the way. Go if you like – my duty is over.'*

Elric, Moonglum and Shaarilla stepped towards the entrance of the castle, but before they entered, the giant spoke warningly from behind them.

'I have been told that the knowledge contained in the Book could swing the balance on the side of the forces of Law. This disturbs me – but, it appears, there is another possibility which disturbs me even more.'

'What is that?' Elric asked.

'It could create such a tremendous impact on the universe that complete entropy would result. My Masters do not desire that – for it could mean the destruction of all matter in the end. We exist only to fight – not to win, but to preserve the eternal struggle.'

'I care not,' Elric told him. 'I have little to lose, Orunlu the Keeper.'

'Then go.' The giant strode across the courtyard into blackness.

Inside the tower, light of a pale quality illuminated winding steps leading upwards. Elric began to climb them in silence, moved by his own doom-filled purpose. Hesitantly, Moonglum and Shaarilla followed in his path, their faces set in hopeless acceptance.

On and upward the steps mounted, twisting tortuously towards their goal, until at last they came to the chamber, full of blinding light, many-coloured and scintillating, which did not penetrate outwards at all but remained confined to the room which housed it.

Blinking, shielding his red eyes with his arm, Elric pressed forward and through slitted pupils saw the source of the light lying on a small stone dais in the centre of the room.

Equally troubled by the bright light, Shaarilla and Moonglum followed him into the room and stood in awe at what they saw.

It was a huge book – the Dead Gods' Book, its covers encrusted with alien gems from which the light sprang. It gleamed, it *throbbed* with light and brilliant colour.

'At last,' Elric breathed. 'At last – the Truth!'

He stumbled forward like a man made stupid with drink, his pale hands reaching for the thing he had sought with such savage bitterness. His hands touched the pulsating cover of the Book and, trembling, turned it back.

'Now, I shall learn,' he said, half-gloatingly.

With a crash, the cover fell to the floor, sending the bright gems skipping and dancing over the paving stones.

Beneath Elric's twitching hands lay nothing but a pile of yellowish dust.

'No!' His scream was anguished, unbelieving. 'No!' Tears flowed down his contorted face as he ran his hands through the fine dust. With a groan which racked his whole being, he fell forward, his face hitting the disintegrated parchment. Time had destroyed the Book – untouched, possibly forgotten, for three hundred centuries. Even the wise and powerful Gods who had created it had perished – and now its knowledge followed them into oblivion, or whatever had awaited them beyond the physical universe.

They stood on the slopes of the high mountain, staring down into the green valleys below them. The sun shone and the sky was clear and blue. Behind them lay the gaping hole which led into the bowels of the earth and the stronghold of the Lords of Entropy on their planet.

Elric looked with sad eyes across the world and his head was lowered beneath the weight of weariness and dark despair which lay upon him. He had not spoken since his companions had dragged him sobbing from the chamber of the Book. Now he raised his head and all the misery of the world showed upon his pale face. He spoke in a voice tinged with self-mockery, sharp with bitterness – a lonely voice like the calling of hungry seabirds circling the cold skies above bleak shores.

'Now,' he said, 'I will live my life without ever knowing why I live it – whether it has purpose or not. Perhaps the Book could have told me. But would I have believed it, even then? I am the eternal sceptic – never *sure* that my actions are my own; never certain that an ultimate entity is not guiding me.

'I envy those who know. All I can do now is to continue my quest and hope, without hope, that before my span is ended, the Truth will be presented to me.'

Shaarilla took his limp hands in hers and her eyes were wet. 'Elric – let me comfort you.'

The albino sneered bitterly. 'Would that we'd never met, Shaarilla of the Dancing Mist. For a while, you gave me hope – I had thought to be at last at peace with myself. But, because of you, I am left more hopeless than before. There is no salvation in this world – only malevolent doom. Goodbye.'

He took his hands away from her grasp and set off down the mountainside.

Moonglum darted a glance at Shaarilla and then at Elric. He took something from his purse and put it in the girl's hand.

'Good luck,' he said, and then he was running after Elric until he caught him up.

Still striding, Elric turned at Moonglum's approach and, despite his brooding misery said: 'What is it, friend Moonglum? Why do you follow me?'

'I've followed you thus far, Master Elric, and I see no reason to stop,' grinned the little man. 'Besides, unlike yourself, I'm a materialist. We'll need to eat, you know.'

Elric frowned, feeling a warmth growing within him. 'What do you mean, Moonglum?'

Moonglum chuckled. 'I take advantage of situations of any kind, where I may,' he answered. He reached into his purse and displayed something on his outstretched hand which shone with a dazzling brilliancy. It was one of the jewels from the cover of the Book. 'There are more in my purse,' he said, 'And each one worth a fortune.' He took Elric's arm.

'Come, Elric – what new lands shall we visit so that we may change these baubles into wine and pleasant company?'

Behind them, still standing stock-still on the hillside, Shaarilla stared miserably after them until they were no longer visible. The jewel Moonglum had given her dropped from her fingers and fell, bouncing and bright, until it was lost amongst the heather. Then she turned – and the dark mouth of the cavern yawned before her.

The Stealer of Souls

1

IN A CITY called Bakshaan, which was rich enough to make all other cities of the North East seem poor, in a tall-towered tavern one night, Elric, Lord of the smoking ruins of Melniboné, smiled like a shark and dryly jested with four powerful merchant princes whom, in a day or so, he intended to pauperize.

Moonglum the Outlander, Elric's companion, viewed the tall albino with admiration and concern. For Elric to laugh and joke was rare – but that he should share his good humour with men of the merchant stamp, that was unprecedented. Moonglum congratulated himself that he was Elric's friend and wondered upon the outcome of the meeting. Elric had, as usual, elaborated little of his plan to Moonglum.

'We need your particular qualities as swordsman and sorcerer, Lord Elric, and will, of course, pay well for them.' Pilarmo, overdressed, intense and scrawny, was main spokesman for the four.

'And how shall you pay, gentlemen?' inquired Elric politely, still smiling.

Pilarmo's colleagues raised their eyebrows and even their spokesman was slightly taken aback. He waved his hand through the smoky air of the tavern-room which was occupied only by the six men.

'In gold – in gems,' answered Pilarmo.

'In chains,' said Elric. 'We free travellers need no chains of that sort.'

Moonglum bent forward out of the shadows where he sat, his expression showing that he strongly disapproved of Elric's statement.

Pilarmo and the other merchants were plainly astonished, too. 'Then how shall we pay you?'

'I will decide that later,' Elric smiled. 'But why talk of such things until the time – what do you wish me to do?'

Pilarmo coughed and exchanged glances with his peers. They nodded. Pilarmo dropped his tone and spoke slowly:

'You are aware that trade is highly competitive in this city, Lord Elric. Many merchants vie with one another to secure the custom of the people. Bakshaan is a rich city and its populace is comfortably off, in the main.'

'This is well known,' Elric agreed; he was privately likening the well-to-do citizens of Bakshaan to sheep and himself to the wolf who would rob the fold. Because of these thoughts, his scarlet eyes were full of a humour which Moonglum knew to be malevolent and ironic.

'There is one merchant in this city who controls more warehouses and shops than any other,' Pilarmo continued. 'Because of the size and strength of his caravans, he can afford to import greater quantities of goods into Bakshaan and thus sell them for lower prices. He is virtually a thief – he will ruin us with his unfair methods.' Pilarmo was genuinely hurt and aggrieved.

'You refer to Nikorn of Ilmar?' Moonglum spoke from behind Elric.

Pilarmo nodded mutely.

Elric frowned. 'This man heads his own caravans – braves the dangers of the desert, forest and mountain. He has earned his position.'

'That is hardly the point,' snapped fat Tormiel, beringed and powdered, his flesh a-quiver.

'No, of course not.' Smooth-tongued Kelos patted his colleague's arm consolingly. 'But we all admire bravery, I hope.' His friends nodded. Silent Deinstaf, the last of the four, also coughed and wagged his hairy head. He put his unhealthy fingers on the jewelled hilt of an ornate but virtually useless poignard and squared his shoulders. 'But,' Kelos went on, glancing at Deinstaf with approval, 'Nikorn takes no risks selling his goods cheaply – he's killing us with his low prices.'

'Nikorn is a thorn in our flesh,' Pilarmo elaborated unnecessarily.

'And you gentlemen require myself and my companion to remove this thorn,' Elric stated.

'In a nutshell, yes.' Pilarmo was sweating. He seemed more than a trifle wary of the smiling albino. Legends referring to

74

Elric and his dreadful, doom-filled exploits were many and elaborately detailed. It was only because of their desperation that they had sought his help in this matter. They needed one who could deal in the nigromantic arts as well as wield a useful blade. Elric's arrival in Bakshaan was potential salvation for them.

'We wish to destroy Nikorn's power,' Pilarmo continued. 'And if this means destroying Nikorn, then –' He shrugged and half-smiled, watching Elric's face.

'Common assassins are easily employed, particularly in Bakshaan,' Elric pointed out softly.

'Uh – true,' Pilarmo agreed. 'But Nikorn employs a sorcerer – and a private army. The sorcerer protects him and his palace by means of magic. And a guard of desert-men serve to ensure that if magic fails, then natural methods can be used for the purpose. Assassins have attempted to eliminate the trader, but unfortunately, they were not lucky.'

Elric laughed. 'How disappointing, my friends. Still, assassins are the most dispensable members of the community – are they not? And their souls probably went to placate some demon who would otherwise have plagued more honest folk.'

The merchants laughed half-heartedly and, at this, Moonglum grinned, enjoying himself from his seat in the shadows.

Elric poured wine for the other five. It was of a vintage which the law in Bakshaan forbade the populace from drinking. Too much drove the imbiber mad, yet Elric had already quaffed great quantities and showed no ill effects. He raised a cup of the yellow wine to his lips and drained it, breathing deeply and with satisfaction as the stuff entered his system. The others sipped theirs cautiously. The merchants were already regretting their haste in contacting the albino. They had a feeling that not only were the legends true – but they did not do justice to the strange-eyed man they wished to employ.

Elric poured more yellow wine into his goblet and his hand trembled slightly and his dry tongue moved over his lips quickly. His breathing increased as he allowed the beverage to trickle down his throat. He had taken more than enough to make other men into mewling idiots, but those few signs were the only indication that the wine had any effect upon him at all.

This was a wine for those who wished to dream of different

75

and less tangible worlds. Elric drank it in the hope that he would, for a night or so, cease to dream.

Now he asked: 'And who is this mighty sorcerer, Master Pilarmo?'

'His name is Theleb K'aarna,' Pilarmo answered nervously.

Elric's scarlet eyes narrowed. 'The sorcerer of Pan Tang?'

'Aye – he comes from that island.'

Elric put his cup down upon the table and rose, fingering his blade of black iron, the runesword *Stormbringer*.

He said with conviction: 'I will help you, gentlemen.' He had made up his mind not to rob them, after all. A new and more important plan was forming in his brain.

'*Theleb K'aarna*,' he thought. '*So you have made Bakshaan your bolt-hole, eh?*'

Theleb K'aarna tittered. It was an obscene sound, coming as it did from the throat of a sorcerer of no mean skill. It did not fit with his sombre, black-bearded countenance, his tall, scarlet-robed frame. It was not a sound suited to one of his extreme wisdom.

Theleb K'aarna tittered and stared with dreamy eyes at the woman who lolled on the couch beside him. He whispered clumsy words of endearment into her ear and she smiled indulgently, stroking his long, black hair as she would stroke the coat of a dog.

'You're a fool, for all your learning, Theleb K'aarna,' she murmured, her hooded eyes staring beyond him at the bright green and orange tapestries which decorated the stone walls of her bed-chamber. She reflected lazily that a woman could not but help take advantage of any man who put himself so into her power.

'Yishana, you are a bitch,' Theleb K'aarna breathed foolishly, 'and all the learning in the world cannot combat love. I love you.' He spoke simply, directly, not understanding the woman who lay beside him. He had seen into the black bowels of hell and had returned sane, he knew secrets which would turn any ordinary man's mind into quivering, jumbled jelly. But in certain arts he was as unversed as his youngest acolyte. The art of love was one of those. 'I love you,' he repeated, and wondered why she ignored him.

Yishana, Queen of Jharkor, pushed the sorcerer away from her and rose abruptly, swinging bare, well-formed legs off the divan. She was a handsome woman, with hair as black as her soul; though her youth was fading, she had a strange evil quality about her which both repelled and attracted men. She wore her multi-coloured silks well and they swirled about her as, with light grace, she strode to the barred window of the chamber and stared out into the dark and turbulent night. The sorcerer watched her through narrow, puzzled eyes, disappointed at this halt to their love-making.

'What's wrong?'

The Queen continued to stare at the night sky. Great banks of black cloud moved like predatory monsters, swiftly across the wind-torn sky. The night was raucous and angry about Bakshaan; full of ominous portent.

Theleb K'aarna repeated his question and again received no answer. He stood up angrily, then, and joined her at the window.

'Let us leave now, Yishana, before it is too late. If Elric learns of our presence in Bakshaan, we shall both suffer.' She did not reply, but her breasts heaved beneath the flimsy fabric and her mouth tightened.

The sorcerer growled, gripping her arm. 'Forget your renegade freebooter Elric – you have me now, and I can do much more for you than any sword-swinging medicine-man from a broken and senile empire!'

Yishana laughed unpleasantly and turned on her lover. 'You are a fool, Theleb K'aarna, and you're much less of a man than Elric. Three aching years have passed since he deserted me, skulking off into the night on your trail and leaving me to pine for him! But I still remember his savage kisses and his wild love-making. Gods! I wish he had an equal. Since he left, I've never found one to match him – though many have tried and proved better than you – until your spells drove them off or destroyed them.' She sneered, mocking and taunting him. 'You've been too long among your parchments to be much good to me!'

The sorcerer's face muscles tautened beneath his tanned skin and he scowled. 'Then why do you let me remain? I could make you my slave with a potion – you know that!'

'But you wouldn't – and are thus *my* slave, mighty wizard.

77

Your calling once forbade you to use your arts against mankind – yet, when Elric threatened to displace you in my affections, you conjured a demon and Elric was forced to fight it. He won, you'll remember – but in his pride refused to compromise. You fled into hiding and he went in search of you – leaving me! That is what you did. You're in *love*, Theleb K'aarna . . . ' she laughed in his face. 'And your love won't let you use your arts against me – only my other lovers. I put up with you because you are often useful, but if Elric were to return . . . '

Theleb K'aarna turned away, pettishly picking at his long black beard. Yishana said: 'I half-hate Elric, aye! But that is better than half-loving you!'

The sorcerer snarled: 'Then why did you join me in Bakshaan? Why did you leave your brother's son upon your throne as regent and come here? I sent word and you came – you must have some affection for me to do that!'

Yishana laughed again. 'I heard that a pale-faced sorcerer with crimson eyes and a howling runesword was travelling in the North East. That is why I came, Theleb K'aarna.'

Theleb K'aarna's face twisted with anger as he bent forward and gripped the woman's shoulder in his taloned hand.

'You'll remember that this same pale-faced sorcerer was responsible for your own brother's death,' he spat. 'You lay with a man who was a slayer of his kin and yours. He deserted the fleet, which he had led to pillage his own land, when the Dragon Masters retaliated. Dharmit, your brother, was aboard one of those ships and he now lies scorched and rotting on the ocean bed.'

Yishana shook her head wearily. 'You always mention this and hope to shame me. Yes, I entertained one who was virtually my brother's murderer – but Elric had ghastlier crimes on his conscience and I still loved him, in spite or because of them. Your words do not have the effect you require, Theleb K'aarna. Now leave me, I wish to sleep alone.'

The sorcerer's nails were still biting into Yishana's cool flesh. He relaxed his grip. 'I am sorry,' he said, his voice breaking. 'Let me stay.'

'Go,' she said softly. And, tortured by his own weakness, Theleb K'aarna, sorcerer of Pan Tang, left. Elric of Melniboné was in Bakshaan – and three years before, Elric had sworn several oaths of vengeance upon Theleb K'aarna. In his heart, the black-bearded sorcerer knew who would win any duel which might take place.

2

The four merchants had left, swathed in dark cloaks. They had not deemed it wise for anyone to be aware of their association with Elric. Now, Elric brooded over a fresh cup of yellow wine. He knew that he would need help of a particular and powerful kind, if he were going to capture Nikorn's castle. It was virtually unstormable and, with Theleb K'aarna's nigromantic protection, a particularly potent sorcery would have to be used. He knew that he was Theleb K'aarna's match and more when it came to wizardry, but if all his energy were expended on fighting the other magician, he would have none left to effect an entry past the crack guard of desert warriors employed by the merchant prince.

He needed help. In the forests which lay to the south of Bakshaan, he knew he would find men whose aid would be useful. But would they help him? He discussed the problem with Moonglum.

'I have heard that a band of my countrymen have recently come north from Vilmir where they have pillaged several large towns,' he informed the Eastlander. 'Since the great battle of Imrryr five years ago, the men of Melniboné have spread outwards from the Dragon Isle, becoming mercenaries and freebooters. It was because of me that Imrryr fell – and this they know, but if I offer them rich loot, they might aid me.'

Moonglum smiled wryly. 'I would not count on it, Elric,' he said. 'Such an act as yours can hardly be forgotten, if you'll forgive my frankness. Your countrymen are now unwilling wanderers, citizens of a razed city – the oldest and greatest the world has known. When Imrryr the Beautiful fell, there must have been many who wished great suffering upon you.'

Elric emitted a short laugh. 'Possibly,' he agreed, 'but these *are* my people and I know them. We Melnibonéans are an old and sophisticated race – we rarely allow emotions to interfere with our general well-being.'

Moonglum raised his eyebrows in an ironic grimace and

79

Elric interpreted the expression rightly. 'I was an exception for a short while,' he said. 'But now Cymoril and my cousin lie in the ruins of Imrryr and my own torment will avenge any ill I have done. I think my countrymen will realise this.'

Moonglum sighed. 'I hope you are right, Elric. Who leads this band?'.

'An old friend,' Elric answered. 'He was Dragon Master and led the attack upon the reaver ships after they had looted Imrryr. His name is Dyvim Tvar, once Lord of the Dragon Caves.'

'And what of his beasts, where are they?'

'Asleep in the caves again. They can be roused only once every century or so – they need years to recuperate while their venom is re-distilled and their energy revitalised. If it were not for this, the Dragon Masters would rule the world.'

'Lucky for you that they don't,' Moonglum commented.

Elric said slowly: 'Who knows? With me to lead them, they might yet. At least, we could carve a new empire from this world, just as our forefathers did.'

Moonglum said nothing. He thought, privately, that the Young Kingdoms would not be so easily vanquished. Melniboné and her people were ancient, cruel and wise – but even their cruelty was tempered with the soft disease which comes with age. They lacked the vitality of the barbarian race who had been the ancestors of the builders of Imrryr and her long-forgotten sister cities. Vitality was often replaced by tolerance – the tolerance of the aged, the ones who have known past glory but whose day is done.

'In the morning,' said Elric, 'we will make contact with Dyvim Tvar and hope that what he did to the reaver fleet, coupled with the conscience-pangs which I have personally suffered, will serve to make his attitude a little less irate.'

'And now, sleep, I think,' Moonglum said. 'I need it, anyway – and the wench who awaits me might be growing impatient.'

Elric shrugged. 'As you will. I'll drink a little more wine and seek my bed later.'

The black clouds which had huddled over Bakshaan on the previous night, were still there in the morning. The sun rose behind them, but the inhabitants were unaware of it. It rose unheralded, but in the fresh, rain-splashed dawn, Elric and Moonglum rode the narrow streets of the city, heading for the south gate and the forests beyond.

Elric had discarded his usual garb for a simple jerkin of green-dyed leather which bore the insignia of the royal line of Melniboné: a scarlet dragon, rampant on a gold field. On his finger was the Ring of Kings, a single rare Actorious stone set in a ring of rune-carved silver. This was the ring that Elric's mighty forefathers had worn; it was many centuries old. A short cloak hung from his shoulders and his hose was also green, tucked into high black riding boots. At his side hung *Stormbringer*, even more ancient than the ring, forged by gods before the world gave birth to human offspring. An evil and terrible sword. A doomed and dreadful symbiosis existed between man and sword – they needed each other. The man without the sword would become a cripple, lacking sight and energy – the sword without the man could not drink the blood and the souls it needed for its existence. They rode together, sword and man, and none could tell which was master.

Moonglum, more conscious of the inclement weather than his friend, hugged a high-collared cloak around him and cursed the elements occasionally.

It took them an hour's hard riding to reach the outskirts of the forest. As yet, in Bakshaan, there were only rumours of the Imrryrian freebooters' coming. Once or twice, a tall stranger had been seen in obscure taverns near the southern wall, and this had been remarked upon but the citizens of Bakshaan felt secure in their wealth and power and had reasoned, with a certain truth in their conviction, that Bakshaan could withstand a raid far more ferocious than those raids which had taken weaker Vilmirian towns. Elric had no idea why his countrymen had driven northwards to Bakshaan. Possibly they had come only to rest and turn their loot into food supplies in the bazaars.

The smoke of several large campfires told Elric and Moonglum where the Melnibonéans were entrenched. With a slackening of pace, they guided their horses in that direction while wet branches brushed their faces and the scents of the forest, released by the life-bringing rain, impinged sweetly upon their nostrils. It was with a feeling akin to relaxation that Elric met the outguard who suddenly appeared from the undergrowth to bar their way along the forest trail.

The Imrryrian guard was swathed in furs and steel. Beneath the visor of an intricately worked helmet he peered at Elric with wary eyes. His vision was slightly impaired by the visor and the rain which dripped from it so that he did not immediately recognise Elric.

'Halt. What do you in these parts?'

Elric said impatiently, 'Let me pass – it is Elric, your lord and your king.'

The guard gasped and lowered the long-bladed spear he carried. He pushed back his helmet and gazed at the man before him with a myriad of different emotions passing across his face. Among these were amazement, reverence and hate.

He bowed stiffly. 'This is no place for you, my liege. You renounced and betrayed your people five years ago and while I acknowledge the blood of kings which flows in your veins, I cannot obey you or do you the homage which it would otherwise be your right to expect.'

'Of course,' said Elric proudly, sitting his horse straight-backed. 'But let your leader – my boyhood friend Dyvim Tvar – be the judge of how to deal with me. Take me to him at once and remember that my companion has done you no ill, but treat him with respect as befits the chosen friend of a King of Melniboné.'

The guard bowed again and took hold of the reins of Elric's mount. He led the pair down the trail and into a large clearing wherein were pitched the tents of the men of Imrryr. Cooking fires flared in the centre of the great circle of pavilions and the fine-featured warriors of Melniboné sat talking softly around them. Even in the light of the gloomy day, the fabrics of the tents were bright and gay. The soft tones were wholly Melnibonéan in texture. Deep, smoky greens, azure, ochre, gold, dark blue. The colours did not clash – they blended. Elric felt sad nostalgia for the sundered, multi-coloured towers of his home-city, Imrryr the Beautiful.

As the two companions and their guide drew nearer, men looked up in astonishment and a low muttering replaced the sounds of ordinary conversation.

'Please remain here,' the guard said to Elric. 'I will inform Lord Dyvim Tvar of your coming.' Elric nodded his acquiescence and sat firmly in his saddle conscious of the gaze of the gathered warriors. None approached him and some, whom Elric had known personally in the old days, were openly embarrassed. They were the ones who did not stare but rather averted their eyes, tending to the cooking fires or taking a sudden interest in the polish of their finely-wrought longswords and dirks. A few growled angrily, but they were in a definite minority. Most of the men were simply shocked – and also inquisitive. Why had this man, their king and their betrayer, come to their camp?

The largest pavilion, of gold and scarlet, had at its peak a banner upon which was emblazoned a dormant dragon, blue upon white. This was the tent of Dyvim Tvar and from it the Dragon Master hurried, buckling on his sword-belt, his intelligent eyes puzzled and wary.

Dyvim Tvar was a man a little older than Elric and he bore the stamp of Melnibonéan nobility. His mother had been a princess, a cousin to Elric's own mother. His cheek-bones were high and delicate, his eyes slightly slanting while his skull was narrow, tapering at the jaw. Like Elric, his ears were thin, near lobeless and coming almost to a point. His hands, the left one now folded around the hilt of his longsword, were long-fingered and, like the rest of his skin, pale, though not nearly so pale as the dead-white of the albino's own skin. He strode towards the mounted King of Melniboné and now his emotions were controlled. When he was five feet away from Elric, Dyvim Tvar bowed slowly, his head bent and his face hidden. When he looked up again, his eyes met those of Elric and remained fixed.

'Dyvim Tvar, Lord of the Dragon Caves, greets King Elric, Master of Melniboné, Exponent of her Secret Arts.' The Dragon Master spoke gravely the age-old ritual greeting.

Elric was not as confident as he seemed as he replied: 'Elric, Master of Melniboné, greets his loyal subject and demands that he give audience to Dyvim Tvar.' It was not fitting, by ancient Melnibonéan standards, that the king should *request* an audience with one of his subjects and the Dragon Master understood this. He now said:

'I would be honoured if my liege would allow me to accom-

83

pany him to my pavilion.'

Elric dismounted and led the way towards Dyvim Tvar's pavilion. Moonglum also dismounted and made to follow, but Elric waved him back. The two Imrryrian noblemen entered the tent.

Inside, a small oil-lamp augmented the gloomy daylight which filtered through the colourful fabric. The tent was simply furnished, possessing only a soldier's hard bed, a table and several carved wooden stools. Dyvim Tvar bowed and silently indicated one of these stools. Elric sat down.

For several moments, the two men said nothing. Neither allowed emotion to register on their controlled features. They simply sat and stared at one another. Eventually Elric said:

'You know me for a betrayer, a thief, a murderer of my own kin and a slayer of my countrymen, Dragon Master.'

Dyvim Tvar nodded. 'With my liege's permission, I will agree with him.'

'We were never so formal in the old days, when alone,' Elric said. 'Let us forget ritual and tradition – Melniboné is broken and her sons are wanderers. We meet, as we used to, as equals – only, now, this is wholly true. We *are* equals. The Ruby Throne crashed in the ashes of Imrryr and now no king may sit in state.'

Dyvim Tvar sighed. 'This is true, Elric – but why have you come here? We were content to forget you. Even while thoughts of vengeance were fresh, we made no move to seek you out. Have you come to mock?'

'You know I would never do that, Dyvim Tvar. I rarely sleep, in these days, and when I do I have such dreams that I would rather be awake. You know that Yyrkoon forced me to do what I did when he put his sister, whom I loved, into a sorcerous slumber. To aid that reaver fleet was my only hope of forcing him to undo his evil work and release his sister Cymoril from the spell. I was moved by vengeance and it was *Storm-bringer*, my sword, which slew Cymoril, not I.'

'Of this, I am aware.' Dyvim Tvar sighed again and rubbed one jewelled hand across his face. 'But it does not explain why you came here. There should be no contact between you and your people. We are wary for you, Elric, for even if we allowed you to lead us again – you would take your own doomed path and us with you. There is no future there for myself and my men.'

'Agreed. But I need your help for just one time – then our ways can part again.'

'We should kill you, Elric. But which would be the greater crime? Failure to do justice and slay our betrayer – or regicide? You have given me a problem at a time when there are too many problems already. Should I attempt to solve it?'

'I but played a part in history,' Elric said earnestly. 'Time would have done what I did, eventually. I but brought the day nearer – and brought it when you and our people were still resilient enough to combat it and turn to a new way of life.'

Dyvim Tvar smiled ironically. 'That is one point of view, Elric – and it has truth in it, I grant you. But tell it to the men who lost their kin and their homes because of you. Tell it to warriors who had to tend maimed comrades, to brothers, fathers and husbands whose wives, daughters and sisters were used to pleasure the reaver pillagers.'

'Aye.' Elric dropped his eyes. When he next spoke it was quietly. 'I can do nothing to replace what our people have lost – would that I could, for I yearn for Imrryr often, and her women, and her wines and entertainments. But I can offer something different. Rich plunder. I can offer you the richest palace in Bakshaan. Forget the old wounds and follow me this once.'

'Do you seek the riches of Bakshaan, Elric? You were never one for jewels and precious metal! Why, Elric?'

'Oh, Gods!' Elric twisted his hands and ran them through his white hair. His red eyes were troubled. 'For vengeance, once again, Dyvim Tvar. I owe a debt to a sorcerer from Pan Tang – Theleb K'aarna. You may have heard of him – he is fairly powerful for one of a comparatively young race.'

'Then we're joined in this, Elric.' Dyvim Tvar spoke grimly. 'You are not the only Melnibonéan who owes Theleb K'aarna a debt! Because of that bitch-queen Yishana of Jharkor, one of our men was done to death a year ago in a most foul and horrible manner. Killed by Theleb K'aarna because he gave his embraces to Yishana. We can unite to avenge that blood, King Elric, and it will be a fitting excuse for those who would rather have your blood on their knives.'

Elric was not glad. He had a sudden premonition that this fortunate coincidence was to have grave and unpredictable outcomings. But he smiled.

3

In a smoking pit of Hell, somewhere beyond the limitations of space and time, a creature stirred. All around it, shadows moved. They were the shadows of the souls of men and these shadows which moved through the bright darkness were the masters of the creature. It allowed them to master it – so long as they paid its price. In the speech of men, this creature had a name. It was called *Quaolnargn* and would answer to this name if called.

Now it stirred. It heard its name carrying over the barriers which normally blocked its way to the Earth. The calling of the name effected a temporary pathway through those intangible barriers. It stirred again, as its name was called for the second time. It was unaware of why it was called or to what it was called. It was only muzzily conscious of one fact. When the pathway was opened to it, it could *feed*. It did not eat flesh and it did not drink blood. It fed on the minds and the souls of adult men and women. Occasionally, as an appetizer, it enjoyed the morsels, the sweetmeats as it were, of the innocent life-force which it sucked from children. It ignored animals since there was not enough *awareness* in an animal to savour. The creature was, for all its alien stupidity, a gourmet and a connoisseur.

Now its name was called for the third time. It stirred again and flowed forward. The time was approaching when it could, once again, *feed* . . .

Theleb K'aarna shuddered. He was, basically, a man of peace. It was not his fault that his avaricious love for Yishana had turned him mad. It was not his fault that, because of her, he had become initiated to the darker side of his chosen profession and now controlled several powerful and malevolent demons who, in return for the slaves and enemies he fed them, protected the palace of Nikorn the merchant. He felt, very strongly, that none of it was his fault. It was circumstance which had damned him. He wished sadly that he had never met Yishana. He shuddered again as he stood within the pentacle and summoned *Quaolnargn*. His embryonic talent for precognition had shown him a little of the near-future and he knew that Elric was preparing to do battle with him. Theleb K'aarna was taking the opportunity of summoning all the aid he could control. *Quaolnargn* must be sent to destroy Elric, if it could, before the albino reached the castle. Theleb K'aarna congratulated himself that he still retained the lock of white hair which had enabled him, in the past, to send another, now deceased, demon against Elric.

Quaolnargn knew that it was reaching its master. It propelled itself sluggishly forward and felt a stinging pain as it entered the alien continuum. It knew that its master's soul hovered before it but, for some reason, was disappointingly unattainable. Something was dropped in front of it. *Quaolnargn* scented at it and knew what it must do. This was part of its new *feed*. It flowed gratefully away, intent on finding its prey before the pain which was endemic of a prolonged stay in the strange place grew too much.

Elric rode at the head of his countrymen. On his right was Dyvim Tvar, the Dragon Master, on his left, Moonglum of Elwher. Behind him rode two hundred fighting men and behind them the wagons containing their loot, their war-machines and their slaves.

The caravan was resplendent with proud banners and the gleaming, long-bladed lances of Imrryr. They were clad in steel, with tapering greaves, helmets and shoulder-pieces. Their breastplates were polished and glinted where their long fur jerkins were open. Over the jerkins were flung bright cloaks of Imrryrian fabrics, scintillating in the watery sunshine. The archers were immediately close to Elric and his companions. They carried unstrung bone bows of tremendous power, which only they could use. On their backs were quivers crammed with black-fletched arrows. Then came the lancers, with their shining lances at a tilt to avoid the low branches of the trees. Behind these rode the main strength – the Imrryrian swordsmen carrying longswords and shorter stabbing weapons which were too short to be real swords and too long to be named as knives.

They rode, skirting Bakshaan, for the palace of Nikorn which lay to the north of Bakshaan. They rode, these men, in silence, They could think of nothing to say while Elric, their liege, led them to battle for the first time in fifteen years.

Stormbringer, the black hellblade, tingled under Elric's hand, anticipating a new sword-quenching. Moonglum fidgeted in his saddle, nervous of the forthcoming fight which he knew would involve dark sorcery. Moonglum had no liking for the sorcerous arts, or for the creatures they spawned. To his mind, men should fight their own battles without help and he knew that Elric agreed with this, though the albino was aware that sorcery could only be combated by sorcery. They rode on, nervous and tense.

Stormbringer shook against Elric's side. A faint moan emanated from the metal and the tone was one of warning. Danger of a demoniac kind was approaching. Elric raised a hand and the cavalcade reined to a halt.

'There is something coming near which only I can deal with,' he informed the men. 'I will ride on ahead.'

He spurred his horse into a wary canter, keeping his eyes before him. *Stormbringer*'s voice was louder, sharper – a muted shriek. The horse trembled and Elric's own nerves were tense. He had not expected any kind of trouble so soon and he prayed that whatever evil was lurking in the forest was not directed against him.

'Arioch, be with me,' he breathed. 'Aid me now, and I'll dedicate a score of desert warriors to you. Aid me, Arioch.'

Arioch was one of the ancient demon-gods of Melniboné – a powerful supernatural who could not be mastered. His aid had to be paid for with blood, souls and fealty. Most of the time he refused that aid.

A foul odour now forced itself into Elric's nostrils. He coughed and covered his mouth with his hands, his eyes darting around him, seeking the source of the stink. The horse whinnied. Elric jumped from the saddle and slapped his mount on the rump, sending it back along the trail. He crouched warily, *Stormbringer* now in his grasp, the black metal quivering from point to pommel.

He sensed it with the witch-sight of his forefathers before he saw it with his eyes. And he recognised its shape. He, himself, was one of its masters. But this time he had no control over *Quaolnargn* – he was standing in no pentacle and his only protection was his blade and his wits. He knew, also, of the power of *Quaolnargn* and shuddered. Could he overcome such a horror single-handedly?

'*Arioch! Arioch! Aid me!*' It was a scream, high and desperate. '*Arioch!*'

There was no time to conjure a spell. *Quaolnargn* was before him, a great green toad-thing which hopped along the trail obscenely, moaning to itself in its Earth-fostered pain. It towered over Elric so that the albino was in its shadow before it was ten feet away from him. Elric breathed quickly and screamed once more: '*Arioch! Blood and souls, if you aid me, now!*'

Suddenly, the toad-demon leapt.

Elric sprang to one side, but was caught by a long-nailed foot which sent him flying into the undergrowth. *Quaolnargn* turned clumsily and its filthy mouth opened hungrily, displaying a deep toothless cavity from which a foul odour poured.

'*Arioch!*'

In its evil and alien insensitivity, the toad-thing did not even recognise the name of so powerful a demon-god. It could not be frightened – it had to be fought.

And as it approached Elric for the second time, the clouds belched rain from their bowels and a downpour lashed the forest.

Half-blinded by the rain smashing against his face, Elric backed behind a tree, his runesword ready. In ordinary terms, *Quaolnargn* was blind. It could not see Elric or the forest. It could not feel the rain. It could only see and smell men's souls – its *feed*. The toad-demon blundered past him and, as it did so, Elric leapt high, holding his blade with both hands, and plunged it to the hilt into the demon's soft and quivering back. Flesh – or whatever Earth-bound stuff formed the demon's body – squelched nauseatingly. Elric pulled at *Stormbringer*'s hilt as the sorcerous sword seared into the hellbeast's back, cutting down where the spine should be but where no spine was. *Quaolnargn* piped its pain. Its voice was thin and reedy, even in such extreme agony. It retaliated.

Elric felt his mind go numb and then his head was filled with a pain which was not natural in any sense. He could not even shriek. His eyes widened in horror as he realised what was happening to him. His soul was being drawn from his body. He knew it. He felt no physical weakness, he was only aware of looking out into . . .

But even that awareness was fading. Everything was fading, even the pain, even the dreadful hell-spawned pain.

'Arioch!' he croaked.

Savagely, he summoned strength from somewhere. Not from himself, not even from *Stormbringer* – from somewhere. Something was aiding him at last, giving him strength – enough strength to do what he must.

He wrenched the blade from the demon's back. He stood over *Quaolnargn*. Above him. He was floating somewhere, not in the air of Earth. Just floating over the demon. With thoughtful deliberation he selected a spot on the demon's skull which he somehow knew to be the only spot on his body where *Stormbringer* might slay. Slowly and carefully, he lowered *Stormbringer* and twisted the runesword through *Quaolnargn*'s skull.

The toad-thing whimpered, dropped – and vanished.

Elric lay sprawled in the undergrowth, trembling the length of his aching body. He picked himself up slowly. All his energy had been drained from him. *Stormbringer*, too, seemed to have lost its vitality, but that, Elric knew would return and, in returning, bring him new strength.

But then he felt his whole frame tugged rigid. He was astounded. What was happening? His senses began to blank out. He had the feeling that he was staring down a long, black tunnel which stretched into nowhere. Everything was vague. He was aware of motion. He was travelling. How – or where, he could not tell.

For brief seconds he travelled, conscious only of an unearthly feeling of motion and the fact that *Stormbringer*, his life, was clutched in his right hand.

Then he felt hard stone beneath him and he opened his eyes – or was it, he wondered, that his vision returned? – and looked up at the gloating face above him.

'Theleb K'aarna,' he whispered hoarsely, 'how did you effect this?'

The sorcerer bent down and tugged *Stormbringer* out of Elric's enfeebled grasp. He sneered. 'I followed your commendable battle with my messenger, Lord Elric. When it was obvious that somehow you had summoned aid – I quickly conjured another spell and brought you here. Now I have your sword and your strength. I know that without it you are nothing. You are in my power, Elric of Melniboné.'

Elric gasped air into his lungs. Gasped it agonisingly, for his whole body was pain-racked. He tried to smile, but it was no good. It was not in his nature to smile when he was beaten. 'Give me back my sword,' he croaked. 'Give it back.'

'We'll have you begging for it yet,' said Theleb K'aarna with a self-satisfied smirk. He chuckled. 'Who talks of vengeance, now, Elric?'

'Give me my sword and you can have your paltry life, scum!' Elric tried to rise but he was too weak. His vision blurred until he could hardly see the gloating sorcerer.

'And what kind of bargain is that?' Theleb K'aarna asked. 'You are not a well man, Lord Elric – and sick men do not bargain. They beg.'

Elric trembled in impotent anger. He tightened his mouth. He would not beg – neither would he bargain. In silence, he glowered at the sorcerer.

'I think what we'll do first,' Theleb K'aarna said smiling, 'is to lock this away.' He hefted *Stormbringer* in his hand and turned towards a cupboard behind him. From his robes he produced a key with which he unlocked the cupboard and placed the runesword inside, carefully locking the door again when he had done so. 'Then, I think, we'll show our virile hero to his ex-mistress – the sister of the man he betrayed five years ago.'

Elric was astonished. 'Yishana – here, in Bakshaan? I did not know.'

'Best that you didn't – best that you didn't.' Theleb K'aarna's chuckle was close to a madman's cackle. 'For the good of both of you, really. Now you shall see your light of love – and she shall see the "man" she has been pining for these three years.'

Elric said nothing.

'After that,' Theleb K'aarna continued, 'my employer

91

Nikorn shall be shown the assassin who thought he could do what others failed to achieve.' He smiled. 'What a day,' he chuckled. 'What a day! So full. So rich with pleasure.'

Theleb K'aarna tittered and picked up a hand-bell. He rang it. A door behind Elric opened and two tall desert warriors strode in. They glanced at Elric and then at Theleb K'aarna. They were evidently amazed.

'No questions,' Theleb K'aarna snapped. 'Take this refuse to the chambers of Queen Yishana.'

Elric fumed as he was hefted up between the two. The men were dark-skinned, bearded and their eyes were deep-set beneath shaggy brows. They wore the heavy wool-trimmed metal caps of their race, and their armour was not of iron but of thick, leather-covered wood. Down a long corridor they lugged Elric's weakened body and one of them rapped sharply on a door.

Elric recognised Ysihana's voice bid them enter. Behind the desert-men and their burden came the tittering, fussing sorcerer. 'A present for you, Yishana,' he called, 'and a nice surprise.'

The desert men entered. Elric could not see Yishana but he heard her gasp. 'On the couch,' directed the sorcerer. Elric was deposited on yielding fabric. He lay completely exhausted on the couch, staring up at a bright, lewd mural which had been painted on the ceiling.

Yishana bent over him. Elric could smell her erotic perfume. He said hoarsely: 'An unprecedented reunion, Queen.' Yishana's eyes were, for a moment, concerned, then they hardened and she laughed cynically.

'Oh – my hero has returned to me at last. But I'd rather he'd come at his own volition, not dragged here by the back of his neck like a puppy. The wolf's teeth have all been drawn and there's no one to savage me at nights.' She turned away, disgust on her painted face. 'Take him away, now, Theleb K'aarna. You have proved your point.'

The sorcerer nodded.

'And now,' he said, 'to visit Nikorn – I think he should be expecting us by this time . . .'

4

Nikorn of Ilmar was not a young man. He was well past fifty but had preserved his youth. His face was that of a peasant, firm-boned but not fleshy. He had the kind of face which, because of its solid bone-structure, does not age much. His eyes were keen and hard as he stared at Elric who had been mockingly propped in a chair.

'So you are Elric of Melniboné, the Wolf of the Sighing Sea, spoiler, reaver and woman-slayer. I think that you could hardly slay a child now. However, I will say that it discomforts me to see any man in such a position – particularly one who has been so active as you. Is it true what the spell-maker says? Were you sent here by my enemies to assassinate me?'

Elric was worrying about his men. What would they do now? Wait – or go on? If they stormed the palace now, then they were doomed – and so was he.

'Is it true?' Nikorn said insistently.

'No,' whispered Elric. 'My quarrel was with Theleb K'aarna. I have an old score to settle with him.'

'I am disinterested in old scores, my friend,' Nikorn said, not unkindly. 'I *am* interested in preserving my life. Who sent you here?'

'Theleb K'aarna speaks falsely if he told you I was sent,' Elric lied. 'I was interested only in paying my debt.'

'It is not only the sorcerer who told me, I'm, afraid,' Nikorn said. 'I have many spies in the city and two of them independently informed me of a plot by local merchants to employ you to kill me.'

Elric smiled faintly. 'Very well,' he agreed. 'It was true, but I had no intention of doing what they asked.'

Nikorn said: 'I might believe you, Elric of Melniboné. But now I do not know what to do with you. I would not turn any-one over to Theleb K'aarna's mercies. May I have your word that you will not make an attempt on my life again?'

'Are we bargaining, Master Nikorn?' Elric said faintly.

'We are.'

'Then what do I give my word in return for, sir?'

'Your life and freedom, Lord Elric.'

'And my sword?'

Nikorn shrugged regretfully. 'I'm sorry – not your sword.'

'Then take my life,' said Elric brokenly.

'Come now – my bargain's good. Have your life and freedom and give your word that you will not plague me again.'

Elric breathed deeply. 'Very well.'

Nikorn moved away. Theleb K'aarna who had been standing in the shadows put a hand on the merchant's arm. 'You're going to release him?'

'Aye,' Nikorn said. 'He's no threat to either of us now.'

Elric was aware of a certain feeling of friendship in Nikorn's attitude towards him. He, too, felt something of the same. Here was a man both courageous and clever. This was how he had risen to the top of his chosen trade. But – Elric fought madness – without *Stormbringer*, what could he do?

The two hundred Imrryrian warriors lay hidden in the undergrowth as dusk gave way to night. They watched and wondered. What had happened to Elric? Was he now in the castle as Dyvim Tvar thought? The Dragon Master was versed in the art of divining, to some extent – as were all members of the royal line of Melniboné. From what small spells he had conjured, it seemed that Elric now lay within the castle walls.

But without Elric to battle the sorcerer's power, how could they take it?

Nikorn's palace was also a fortress, bleak and unlovely. It was surrounded by a deep moat of dark, stagnant water. It stood high above the surrounding forest, built *into* rather than *on to* the rock. Much of it had been carved out of the living stone. It was sprawling and rambling and covered a large area, surrounded by natural buttresses. The rock was porous in places, and slimy water ran down the walls of the lower parts, spreading through dark moss. It was not a pleasant place, judging from the outside, but it was almost certainly impregnable. Two hundred men could not take it, without the aid of magic.

Some of the Melnibonéan warriors were becoming impatient. There were a few who muttered that Elric had, once again, betrayed them. Dyvim Tvar and Moonglum did not believe this. They had seen the signs of conflict – and heard them –

in the forest.

They waited. Hoping for a signal from the castle itself.

They watched the castle's great main gate – and their patience was at last proved to be of value. The huge wood and metal gate swung inwards on chains and a white-faced man in the tattered regalia of Melniboné appeared between two desert warriors. They were supporting him, it seemed. They pushed him forward – he staggered a few yards along the causeway of slimy stone which bridged the moat.

Then he fell. He began to crawl wearily, painfully, forward.

Moonglum growled. 'What have they done to him? I must help him.' But Dyvim Tvar held him back.

'No – it would not do to betray our presence here. Let him reach the forest first, then we can help him.'

Even those who had cursed Elric, now felt pity for the albino as, staggering and crawling alternately, he dragged his body slowly towards them. From the battlements of the fortress a tittering laugh was borne, like the cry of a seabird, down to the ears of those below. They also caught a few words.

'*What now, wolf?*' said the voice. '*What now?*'

Moonglum clenched his hands and trembled with rage, hating to see his proud friend so mocked in his weakness. 'What's happened to him? What have they done?'

'Patience,' Dyvim Tvar said. 'We'll find out in a short while.'

It was an agony to wait until Elric finally crawled on his knees into the undergrowth.

Moonglum went forward to aid his friend. He put a supporting arm around Elric's shoulders but the albino snarled and shook it off, his whole countenance aflame with terrible hate – made more terrible because it was impotent. Elric could do nothing to destroy that which he hated. Nothing.

Dyvim Tvar said urgently: 'Elric, you must tell us what happened. If we're to help you – we must know what happened.'

Elric breathed heavily and nodded his agreement. His face partially cleared of the emotion he felt and weakly he stuttered out the story.

'So,' Moonglum growled, 'our plans come to nothing – and you have lost your strength for ever.'

Elric shook his head. 'There must be a way,' he gasped. 'There must!'

95

'What? How? If you have a plan, Elric – let me hear it now.'

Elric swallowed thickly and mumbled. 'Very well, Moonglum, you shall hear it. But listen carefully, for I have not the strength to repeat it.'

Moonglum was a lover of the night, but only when it was lit by the torches found in cities. He did not like the night when it came to open countryside and he was not fond of it when it surrounded a castle such as Nikorn's, but he pressed on and hoped for the best.

If Elric had been right in his interpretation, then the battle might yet be won and Nikorn's palace taken. But it still meant danger for Moonglum and he was not one to deliberately put himself into danger. Moonglum felt that his selfless actions were definite proof of his friendship for the albino.

As he viewed the stagnant waters of the moat with distaste he reflected that this was enough to test any friendship to the utmost. Philosophically, he lowered himself down into the water and began to swim across it.

The moss on the fortress offered a flimsy handhold, but it led to ivy which gave a better grip. Moonglum slowly clambered up the wall. He hoped that Elric had been right and that Theleb K'aarna would need to rest for a while before he could work more sorcery. That was why Elric had suggested he make haste. Moonglum clambered on, and eventually reached the small unbarred window he sought. A normal-size man could not have entered, but Moonglum's small frame was proving useful.

He wriggled through the gap, shivering with cold, and landed on the hard stone of a narrow staircase which ran both up and down the interior wall of the fortress. Moonglum frowned, and then took the steps leading upwards. Elric had given him a rough idea of how to reach his destination.

Expecting the worst, he went soft-footed up the stone steps. He went towards the chambers of Yishana, Queen of Jharkor.

In an hour, Moonglum was back, shivering with cold and dripping with water. In his hands he carried *Stormbringer*. He carried the runesword with cautious care – nervous of its sentient evil. It was alive again; alive with black, pulsating life.

'Thank the gods I was right,' Elric murmured weakly from where he lay surrounded by two or three Imrryrians, including Dyvim Tvar who was staring at the albino with concern. 'I prayed that I was correct in my assumption and Theleb K'aarna was resting after his earlier exertions on my behalf . . . '

He stirred, and Dyvim Tvar helped him to sit upright. Elric reached out a long white hand – reached like an addict of some terrible drug towards the sword. 'Did you give her my message?' he asked as he gratefully seized the pommel.

'Aye,' Moonglum said shakily, 'and she agreed. You were also right in your other interpretation, Elric. It did not take her long to inveigle the key out of a weary Theleb K'aarna. The sorcerer was tremendously tired and Nikorn was becoming nervous, wondering if an attack of any kind would take place while Theleb K'aarna was incapable of action. She went herself to the cupboard and got me the blade.'

'Women can sometimes be useful,' said Dyvim Tvar dryly. 'Though usually, in matters like these, they're a hindrance.' It was possible to see that something other than immediate problems of taking the castle were worrying Dyvim Tvar, but no one thought to ask him what it was that bothered him. It seemed a personal thing.

'I agree, Dragon Master,' Elric said, almost gaily. The gathered men were aware of the strength which poured swiftly back into the albino's deficient veins, imbuing him with a new hell-born vitality. 'It is time for our vengeance. But remember – no harm to Nikorn. I gave him my word.'

He folded his right hand firmly around *Stormbringer's* hilt. 'Now for a sword-quenching. Arioch, Demon God of Melniboné, is with us. He needs me, particularly, to pay what I owe him for his help in the last battle I had with Theleb K'aarna's puny spawning. Now, we shall deal with Theleb K'aarna. I believe I can obtain the help of just the allies we need to keep the sorcerer occupied while we storm the castle. I'll need no pentacle to summon my friends of the air!'

Moonglum licked his long lips. 'So it's sorcery again. In truth, Elric, this whole country is beginning to stink of wizardry and the minions of Hell.'

Elric murmured for his friend's ears: 'No Hell-beings these – but honest elementals, cleaner and more wholesome than the scum of Hell, but equally as powerful in many ways. Curb your belly-fear, Moonglum – a little more simple conjuring and Theleb K'aarna will have no desire to retaliate against me again.'

The albino frowned, remembering the secret pacts of his forefathers. He took a deep breath and closed his pain-filled scarlet eyes. He swayed, the runesword half-loose in his grip. His chant was low, like the far-off moaning of the wind itself. His chest moved quickly up and down, and some of the younger warriors, those who had never been fully initiated into the ancient lore of Melniboné, stirred with discomfort. Elric's voice was not addressing human folk – his words were for the invisible, the intangible – the supernatural. An old and ancient rhyme began the casting of word-runes . . .

> '*Hear the doomed one's dark decision,*
> *Let the Wind Giant's wail be heard,*
> *Graoll and Misha's mighty moaning*
> *Send my enemy like a bird.*

> '*By the sultry scarlet stones,*
> *By the bane of my black blade,*
> *By the Lasshaar's lonely mewling,*
> *Let a mighty wind be made.*

> '*Speed of sunbeams from their homeland,*
> *Swifter than the sundering storm,*
> *Speed of arrow deerwards shooting,*
> *Let the sorcerer so be borne.*'

His voice broke and he called high and clear:
'*Misha! Misha! In the name of my fathers I summon thee, Lord of the Winds!*'

Almost at once, the trees of the forest suddenly bent as if some great hand had brushed them aside. A terrible soughing voice swam from nowhere. And all but Elric, deep in his trance, shivered.

'ELRIC OF MELINBONÉ,' the voice roared like a distant storm, 'I KNEW YOUR FATHERS. I KNOW THEE. THE DEBT WE OWE THE LINE OF ELRIC IS FORGOTTEN BY MORTALS BUT GRAOLL AND

The voice seemed almost friendly – but proud and aloof and
awe-inspiring.

Elric, completely in a state of trance now, jerked his whole
body in convulsions. His voice shrieked piercingly from his
throat – and the words were alien, inhuman, violently disturbing to the ears and nerves of the human listeners. Elric
spoke briefly and then the invisible Wind Giant's great voice
roared and sighed:

'I WILL DO AS YOU DESIRE.' Then the trees bent once more and
the forest was still and muted.

Somewhere in the gathered ranks, a man sneezed sharply,
and this was a sign for others to start talking – speculating.

For many moments, Elric remained in his trance and then,
quite suddenly, he opened his enigmatic eyes and looked
gravely around him, puzzled for a second. Then he clasped
Stormbringer more firmly and leaned forward, speaking to the
men of Imrryr. 'Soon Theleb K'aarna will be in our power, my
friends, and so also will we possess the loot of Nikorn's palace!'

The men growled their bloodlust and even Moonglum
became excited at the prospect of the mighty siege ahead of
them.

But Dyvim Tvar shuddered then. 'I'm not so given to the
esoteric arts as you, Elric,' he said quietly. 'But in my soul I see
three wolves leading a pack to slaughter and one of those
wolves must die. My doom is near me, I think.'

Elric said uncomfortably: 'Worry not, Dragon Master.
You'll live to mock the ravens and spend the spoils of Bakshaan.' But his voice was not entirely convincing, even to his
own ears.

5

In his bed of silk and ermine, Theleb K'aarna stirred and
awoke. He had a brooding inkling of coming trouble and he
remembered that earlier in his tiredness he had given more to
Yishana than had been wise. He could not remember what it
was and now he had a presentiment of danger – the closeness of
which overshadowed thoughts of any past indiscretion. He

arose hurriedly and pulled his robe over his head, shrugged into it as he walked towards a strangely-silvered mirror which was set on one wall of his chamber and reflected no image.

With bleary eyes and trembling hands he began preparations. From one of the many earthenware jars resting on a bench near the window, he poured a substance which seemed like dried blood mottled with the hardened blue venom of the black serpent whose homeland was in far Dorel which lay on the edge of the world. Over this, he muttered a swift incantation, scooped the stuff into a crucible and hurled it at the mirror, one arm shielding his eyes. A crack sounded, hard and sharp to his ears, and bright green light erupted suddenly and was gone. The mirror flickered deep within itself, the silvering seemed to undulate and flicker and flash and then a picture began to form.

Theleb K'aarna knew that the sight he witnessed had taken place in the recent past. It showed him Elric's summoning of the Wind Giants.

Theleb K'aarna's dark features grinned with a terrible fear. His hands jerked as spasms shook him. Half-gibbering, he rushed back to his bench and, leaning his hands upon it, stared out of the window into the deep night. He knew what to expect.

A great and dreadful storm was blowing – and he was the object of the Lasshaar's attack. He *had* to retaliate, else his own soul would be wrenched from him by the Giants of the Wind and flung to the air spirits, to be borne for eternity on the winds of the world. Then his voice would moan like a banshee around the cold peaks of high ice-clothed mountains for ever – lost and lonely. His soul would be damned to travel with the four winds wherever their caprice might bear it, knowing no rest.

Theleb K'aarna had a respect born of fear for the powers of the aeromancer, the rare wizard who could control the wind elementals – and aeromancy was only one of the divining arts which Elric and his ancestors possessed. Then Theleb K'aarna realised what he was battling – ten thousand years and hundreds of generations of sorcerers who had gleaned knowledge from the Earth and beyond it and passed it down to the albino whom he, Theleb K'aarna, had sought to destroy. Then Theleb K'aarna fully regretted his actions. Then – it was too late.

The sorcerer had no control over the powerful Wind Giants

as Elric had. His only hope was to combat one element with another. The fire-spirits must be summoned, and quickly. All of Theleb K'aarna's pyromantic powers would be required to hold off the ravening supernatural winds which were soon to shake the air and the earth. Even Hell would shake to the sound and the thunder of the Wind Giants' wrath.

Quickly, Theleb K'aarna marshalled his thoughts and, with trembling hands, began to make strange passes in the air and promise unhealthy pacts with whichever of the powerful fire elementals would help him this once. He promised himself to eternal death for the sake of a few more years of life.

With the gathering of the Wind Giants came the thunder and the rain. The lightning flashed sporadically, but not lethally. It never touched the earth. Elric, Moonglum, and the men of Imrryr were aware of disturbing movements in the atmosphere, but only Elric with his witch sight could see a little of what was happening. The Lasshaar Giants were invisible to other eyes.

The war engines which the Imrryrians were even now con-structing from pre-fashioned parts were puny things compared to the Wind Giants' might. But victory depended upon these engines since the Lasshaar's fight would be with the super-natural not the natural.

Battle-rams and siege ladders were slowly taking shape as the warriors worked with frantic speed. The hour of the storming came closer as the wind rose and thunder rattled. The moon was blanked out by huge billowings of black cloud, and the men worked by the light of torches. Surprise was no great asset in an attack of the kind planned.

Two hours before dawn, they were ready.

At last the men of Imrryr, Elric, Dyvim Tvar and Moonglum riding high at their head, moved towards the castle of Nikorn. As they did so, Elric raised his voice in an unholy shout – and thunder rumbled in answer to him. A great gout of lightning seared out of the sky towards the palace and the whole place shook and trembled as a ball of mauve and orange fire suddenly appeared over the castle and *absorbed* the lightning! The battle between fire and air had begun.

The surrounding countryside was alive with a weird and malignant shrieking and moaning, deafening to the ears of the marching men. They sensed conflict all round them, and only a little was visible.

Over most of the castle an unearthly glow hung, waxing and waning, defending a gibbering wretch of a sorcerer who knew that he was doomed if once the Lords of the Flame gave way to the roaring Wind Giants.

Elric smiled without humour as he observed the war. On the supernatural plane, he now had little to fear. But there was still the castle and he had no extra supernatural aid to help him take that. Swordplay and skill in battle was the only hope against the ferocious desert warriors who now crowded the battlements, preparing to destroy the two hundred men who came against them.

Up rose the Dragon Standards, their cloth-of-gold fabric flashing in the eerie glow. Spread out, walking slowly, the sons of Imrryr moved forward to do battle. Up, also, rose the siege ladders as captains directed warriors to begin the assault. The defenders' faces were pale spots against the dark stone and thin shouts came from them; but it was impossible to catch their words.

Two great battle-rams, fashioned the day before, were brought to the vanguard of the approaching warriors. The narrow causeway was a dangerous one to pass over, but it was the only means of crossing the moat at ground level. Twenty men carried each of the great iron-tipped rams and now they began to run forward while arrows hailed downwards. Their shields protecting them from most of the shafts, the warriors reached the causeway and rushed across it. Now the first ram connected with the gate. It seemed to Elric as he watched this operation that nothing of wood and iron could withstand the vicious impact of the ram, but the gates shivered almost imperceptibly – and held!

Like vampires, hungry for blood, the men howled and staggered aside crabwise to let pass the log held by their comrades. Again the gates shivered, more easily noticed this time, but they yet held.

Dyvim Tvar roared encouragement to those now scaling the siege ladders. These were brave, almost desperate men, for few of the first climbers would reach the top and even if they were successful, they would be hard-pressed to stay alive until their comrades arrived.

Boiling lead hissed from great cauldrons set on spindles so that they could be easily emptied and filled quickly. Many a brave Imrryrian warrior fell earthwards, dead from the searing metal before he reached the sharp rocks beneath. Large stones were released out of leather bags hanging from rotating pulleys which could swing out beyond the battlements and rain bone-crushing death on the besiegers. But still the invaders advanced, voicing half-a-hundred war-shouts and steadily scaling their long ladders, whilst their comrades, using a shield barrier still, to protect their heads, concentrated on breaking down the gates.

Elric and his two companions could do little to help the scalers or the rammers at that stage. All three were hand-to-hand fighters, leaving even the archery to their rear ranks of bowmen who stood in rows and shot their shafts high into the castle defenders.

The gates were beginning to give. Cracks and splits appeared in them, ever widening. Then, all at once, when hardly expected, the right gate creaked on tortured hinges and fell. A triumphant roar erupted from the throats of the invaders and, dropping their hold on the logs, they led their companions through the breach, axes and maces swinging like scythes and flails before them – and enemy heads springing from necks like wheat from the stalk.

'The castle is ours!' shouted Moonglum, running forward and upward towards the gap in the archway. 'The castle's taken.'

'Speak not too hastily of victory,' replied Dyvim Tvar, but he laughed as he spoke and ran as fast as the others to reach the castle.

'And where is your doom, now?' Elric called to his fellow Melnibonéan, then broke off sharply when Dyvim Tvar's face clouded and his mouth set grimly. For a moment there was tension between them, even as they ran, then Dyvim Tvar laughed loud and made a joke of it. 'It lies somewhere, Elric, it lies somewhere – but let us not worry about such things, for if my doom hangs over me, I cannot stop its descent when my hour arrives!' He slapped Elric's shoulder, feeling for the albino's uncharacteristic confusion.

Then they were under the mighty archway and in the court-yard of the castle where savage fighting had developed almost into single duels, enemy choosing enemy and fighting him to the death.

Stormbringer was the first of the three men's blades to take blood and send a desert man's soul to Hell. The song it sang as it was lashed through the air in strong strokes was an evil one – evil and triumphant.

The dark-faced desert warriors were famous for their courage and skill with swords. Their curved blades were reaping havoc in the Imrryrian ranks for, at that stage, the desert men far outnumbered the Melnibonéan force.

Somewhere above, the inspired scalers had got a firm foot-hold on the battlements and were closing with the men of Nikorn, driving them back, forcing many over the unrailed edges of the parapets. A falling, still screaming warrior plummeted down, to land almost on Elric, knocking his shoulder and causing him to fall heavily to the blood-and-rain-slick cobbles. A badly scarred desert man, quick to see his chance, moved forward with a gloating look on his travesty of a face. His scimitar moved up, poised to hack Elric's neck from his shoulders, and then his helmet split open and his forehead spurted a sudden gout of blood.

Dyvim Tvar wrenched a captured axe from the skull of the slain warrior and grinned at Elric as the albino rose.

'We'll both live to see victory, yet!' he shouted over the din of the warring elementals above them and the sound of clashing arms. 'My doom, I will escape until – ' He broke off, a look of surprise on his fine-boned face, and Elric's stomach twisted inside him as he saw a steel point appear in Dyvim Tvar's right side. Behind the Dragon Master, a maliciously smiling desert warrior pulled his blade from Dyvim Tvar's body. Elric cursed and rushed forward. The man put up his blade to defend himself, backing hurriedly away from the infuriated albino. *Stormbringer* swung up and then down, it howled a death-song and sheared right through the curved steel of Elric's opponent – and it kept on going, straight through the man's shoulder blade, splitting him in two. Elric turned back to Dyvim Tvar who was still standing up, but was pale and strained. His blood dripped from his wound and seeped through his garments.

'How badly are you hurt?' Elric asked anxiously. 'Can you tell?'

'That trollspawn's sword passed through my ribs, I think – no vitals were harmed.' Dyvim Tvar gasped and tried to smile. 'I'm sure I'd know if he'd made more of the wound.'

Then he fell. And when Elric turned him, he looked into a dead and staring face. The Dragon Master, Lord of the Dragon Caves, would never tend his beasts again.

Elric felt sick and weary as he got up, standing over the body of his kinsman. Because of me, he thought, another fine man has died. But this was the only conscious thought he allowed himself for the meantime. He was forced to defend himself from the slashing swords of a couple of desert men who came at him in a rush.

The archers, their work done outside, came running through the breach in the gate and their arrows poured into the enemy ranks.

Elric shouted loudly: 'My kinsman Dyvim Tvar lies dead, stabbed in the back by a desert warrior – avenge him brethren. Avenge the Dragon Master of Imrryr!'

A low moaning came from the throats of the Melnibonéans and their attack was even more ferocious than before. Elric called to a bunch of axe-men who ran down from the battlements, their victory assured.

'You men, follow me. We can avenge the blood that Theleb K'aarna took!' He had a good idea of the geography of the castle.

Moonglum shouted from somewhere. 'One moment, Elric, and I'll join you!' A desert warrior fell, his back to Elric, and from behind him emerged a grinning Moonglum, his sword covered in blood from point to pommel.

Elric led the way to a small door, set into the main tower of the castle. He pointed at it and spoke to the axe-men. 'Set to with your axes, lads, and hurry!'

Grimly, the axe-men began to hack at the tough timber. Impatiently, Elric watched as the wood chips started to fly.

The conflict was appalling. Theleb K'aarna sobbed in frustration. Kakatal, the Fire Lord, and his minions were having little effect on the Wind Giants. Their power appeared to be increasing if anything. The sorcerer gnawed his knuckles and quaked in his chamber while below him the human warriors fought, bled and died. Theleb K'aarna made himself concentrate on one thing only – total destruction of the Lasshaar forces. But he knew, somehow, even then, that sooner or later, in one way or another, he was doomed.

The axes drove deeper and deeper into the stout timber. At last it gave. 'We're through, King Elric,' one of the axe-men indicated the gaping hole they'd made.

Elric reached his arm through the gap and prised up the bar which secured the door. The bar moved upwards and then fell with a clatter to the stone flagging. Elric put his shoulder to the door and pushed.

Above them, now, two huge, almost-human figures had appeared in the sky, outlined against the night. One was golden and glowing like the sun and seemed to wield a great sword of fire. The other was dark blue and silver, writhing, smoke-like, with a flickering spear of restless orange in his hand.

Misha and Kakatal clashed. The outcome of their mighty struggle might well decide Theleb K'aarna's fate.

'Quickly,' Elric said. 'Upwards!'

They ran up the stairs. The stairs which led to Theleb K'aarna's chamber.

Suddenly the men were forced to stop as they came to a door of jet-black, studded with crimson iron. It had no keyhole, no bolts, no bars, but it was quite secure. Elric directed the axe-men to begin hewing at it. All six struck at the door in unison.

In unison, they screamed and vanished. Not even a wisp of smoke remained to mark where they had disappeared.

Moonglum staggered backwards, eyes wide in fear. He was backing away from Elric who remained firmly by the door, *Stormbringer* throbbing in his hand. 'Get out, Elric – this is a sorcery of terrible power. Let your friends of the air finish the wizard!'

Elric shouted half-hysterically: 'Magic is best fought by magic!' He hurled his whole body behind the blow which he struck at the black door. *Stormbringer* whined into it, shrieked as if in victory and howled like a soul-hungry demon. There was a blinding flash, a roaring in Elric's ears, a sense of weight-

106

lessness; and then the door had crashed inwards. Moonglum witnessed this – he had remained against his will.

'*Stormbringer* has rarely failed me, Moonglum,' cried Elric as he leapt through the aperture. 'Come, we have reached Theleb K'aarna's den – ' He broke off, staring at the gibbering thing on the floor. It had been a man. It had been Theleb K'aarna. Now it was hunched and twisted – sitting in the middle of a broken pentacle and tittering to itself.

Suddenly, intelligence came into its eyes. 'Too late for vengeance, Lord Elric,' it said. 'I have won, you see – I have claimed your vengeance as my own.'

Grim-faced and speechless, Elric stepped forward, lifted *Stormbringer* and brought the moaning runesword down into the sorcerer's skull. He left it there for several moments.

'Drink your fill, hell-blade,' he murmured. 'We have earned it, you and I.'

Overhead, there was a sudden silence.

6

'It's untrue! You lie!' screamed the frightened man. 'We were not responsible.' Pilarmo faced the group of leading citizens. Behind the overdressed merchant were his three colleagues – those who had earlier met Elric and Moonglum in the tavern.

One of the accusing citizens pointed a chubby finger towards the north and Nikorn's palace.

'So – Nikorn was an enemy of all other traders in Bakshaan. That I accept. But now a horde of bloody-handed reavers attack his castle with the aid of demons – and Elric of Melniboné leads them! You know that you were responsible – the gossip's all over the city. You employed Elric – and this is what's happened!'

'But we didn't know he would go to such lengths to kill Nikorn!' Fat Tormiel wrung his hands, his face aggrieved and afraid. 'You are wronging us. We only . . . '

'We're wronging *you*!' Faratt, spokesman for his fellow citizens, was thick-lipped and florid. He waved his hands in angry exasperation. 'When Elric and his jackals have done with Nikorn – they'll come to the city. Fool! That is what the albino sorcerer planned to begin with. He was only mocking you – for you provided him with an excuse. Armed men we can fight – but not foul sorcery!'

'What shall we do? What shall we do? Bakshaan will be razed within the day!' Tormiel turned on Pilarmo. 'This was your idea – you think of a plan!'

Pilarmo stuttered: 'We could pay a ransom – bribe them – give them enough money to satisfy them.'

'And who shall give this money?' asked Faratt.

Again the argument began.

Elric looked with distaste at Theleb K'aarna's broken corpse. He turned away and faced a blanch-featured Moonglum who said hoarsely: 'Let's away, now, Elric. Yishana awaits you in Bakshaan as she promised. You must keep your end of the bargain I made for you.'

Elric nodded wearily. 'Aye – the Imrryrians seem to have taken the castle by the sound of it. We'll leave them to their spoiling and get out while we may. Will you allow me a few moments here, alone?'

Moonglum sighed thankfully, incredulous though he was of Elric's uncharacteristic courtesy. 'I'll join you in the courtyard within the quarter hour. I wish to claim some measure of the spoils.' He left, clattering cheerfully down the stairs while Elric remained standing over his enemy's body. He spread out his arms, the sword, dripping blood, still in his hand.

'Dyvim Tvar,' he cried. 'Dyvim Tvar. You and our country-men have been avenged. Let any evil one who holds the soul of Dyvim Tvar release it now and take instead the soul of Theleb K'aarna.'

Within the room something invisible and intangible – but sensed all the same – flowed and hovered over the sprawled body of Theleb K'aarna. Elric looked out of the window and thought he heard the beating of dragon wings – smelled the acrid breath of dragons – saw a shape winging across the dawn sky bearing Dyvim Tvar the Dragon Master away to a land where dragons never slumbered and where myriad dimensions blended under a never-setting sun.

Elric half-smiled. 'The Gods of Melniboné protect thee wherever thou art,' he said quietly and turned away from the carnage, leaving the room.

On the stairway, he met Nikorn of Ilmar.

The merchant's rugged face was full of anger. He trembled with rage. There was a big sword in his hand.

'So I've found you, wolf,' he said. 'I gave you your life – and you have done this to me!'

Elric said tiredly: 'It was to be. But I gave my word that I would not take your life and, believe me, I would not, Nikorn, even had I not pledged my word.'

Nikorn stood two steps from the door blocking the exit. 'Then I'll take yours. Come – engage!' He moved out into the courtyard, half-stumbled over an Imrryrian corpse, righted himself and waited, glowering, for Elric to emerge. Elric did so, his runesword sheathed.

'No.'

'Defend yourself, wolf!'

Automatically, the albino's right hand crossed to his sword hilt, but he still did not unsheath it. Nikorn cursed and aimed a well-timed blow which barely missed the white-faced sorcerer. He skipped back and now he tugged out *Stormbringer*, still reluctant, and stood poised and wary, waiting for the Bakshaanite's next move.

Elric intended simply to disarm Nikorn. He did not want to kill or maim this brave man who had spared him when he had been entirely at the other's mercy.

Nikorn swung another powerful stroke at Elric and the albino parried. *Stormbringer* was moaning softly, shuddering and pulsating. Metal clanged and then the fight was on in full earnest as Nikorn's rage turned to calm, possessed fury. Elric was forced to defend himself with all his skill and power. Though older than the albino, and a city merchant, Nikorn was a superb swordsman. His speed was fantastic and, at times, Elric was not on the defensive only because he desired it.

But something was happening to the runeblade. It was twisting in Elric's hand and forcing him to make a counter-attack. Nikorn backed away – a light akin to fear in his eyes as he realised the potency of Elric's hell-forged steel. The merchant fought grimly and Elric did not fight at all. He felt entirely in the power of the whining sword which hacked and cut at Nikorn's guard.

Stormbringer suddenly shifted in Elric's hand. Nikorn screamed. The runesword left Elric's grasp and plunged on its own accord towards the heart of his opponent.

'No!' Elric tried to catch hold of his blade but could not. *Stormbringer* plunged into Nikorn's great heart and wailed in demoniac triumph. 'No!' Elric got hold of the hilt and tried to pull it from Nikorn. The merchant shrieked in hell-brought agony. He should have been dead.

He still half-lived.

'It's taking me – the thrice-damned thing is taking me!' Nikorn gurgled horribly, clutching at the black steel with hands turned to claws. 'Stop it, Elric – I beg you, stop it! *Please!*'

Elric tried again to tug the blade from Nikorn's heart. He could not. It was rooted in flesh, sinew and vitals. It moaned greedily, drinking into it all that was the being of Nikorn of Ilmar. It sucked the life-force from the dying man and all the while its voice was soft and disgustingly sensuous. Still Elric struggled to pull the sword free. It was impossible. 'Damn you!' he moaned. 'This man was almost my friend – I gave him my word not to kill him.' But *Stormbringer*, though sentient, could not hear its master.

Then Nikorn shrieked once more, the shriek dying to a low, lost whimper. And then his body died.

It died – and the soul-stuff of Nikorn joined the souls of the countless others, friends, kin and enemies who had gone to feed that which fed Elric of Melniboné.

Elric sobbed.

'Gods of Melniboné – why is this curse upon me? Why?'

He collapsed to the ground in the dirt and the blood.

Minutes later, Moonglum came upon his friend lying face downward. He grasped Elric by his shoulder and turned him. He shuddered when he saw the albino's agony-racked face.

'What happened?'

Elric raised himself on one elbow and pointed to where Nikorn's body lay a few feet away. 'Another, Moonglum. I've done it once again. Oh, curse this blade!'

Moonglum said uncomfortably: 'He would have killed you no doubt. Do not think about it. Many a word's been broken through no fault of he who gave it. Come, my friend, Yishana awaits us in the Tavern of the Purple Dove. Come.'

Elric struggled upright and began to walk slowly towards the battered gates of the palace where horses awaited them.

As they rode for Bakshaan, not knowing what concern was troubling the people of that city, Elric tapped *Stormbringer* which hung, once more, at his side. His eyes were hard and moody, turned inwards on his own feelings.

'Be wary of this devil-blade, Moonglum. It kills the foe – but savours the blood of friends and kin-folk most.'

Moonglum shook his head quickly, as if to clear it, and looked away. He said nothing.

Elric made as if to speak again but then changed his mind. He needed to talk, then. He needed to – but there was nothing to say at all.

Pilarmo scowled. He stared, hurt-faced, as his slaves struggled with his chests of treasure, lugging them out to pile them in the street beside his great house. In other parts of the city, Pilarmo's three colleagues were also in various stages of heart-break. Their treasure, too, was being dealt with in a like manner. The burghers of Bakshaan had decided who was to pay any possible ransom.

And then a ragged citizen was shambling down the street, pointing behind him and shouting.

'The albino and his companion – at the North gate. They're coming! Elric comes!'

The burghers who stood near to Pilarmo exchanged glances. Faratt swallowed.

He said: 'Elric comes to bargain. Quick. Open the treasure chests and tell the city guard to admit him through the gate.' One of the citizens scurried off.

Within a few minutes, while Faratt and the rest worked frantically to expose Pilarmo's treasure to the gaze of the approaching albino, Elric was galloping up the street, Moonglum beside him. Both men were expressionless. They knew enough not to show their puzzlement.

'What's this?' Elric asked, casting a look at Pilarmo.

Faratt cringed. 'Treasure,' he whined. 'Yours, Lord Elric – for you and your men. There's much more. There is no need to use sorcery. No need for your men to attack us. The treasure

111

here is fabulous – its value is enormous. Will you take it and leave the city in peace?'

Moonglum almost smiled, but he controlled his features.

Elric said coolly: 'It will do. Very well, I accept – but make sure this and the rest is delivered to my men at Nikorn's castle or we'll be roasting you and your friends over open fires by the morrow.'

Faratt coughed suddenly, trembling. 'As you say, Lord Elric. It shall be delivered.'

The two men wheeled their horses in the direction of the Tavern of the Purple Dove. When they were out of earshot Moonglum said: 'From what I gathered, back there, it's Master Pilarmo and his friends who are paying that unasked-for toll.'

Elric was incapable of any real humour, but he half-chuckled. 'Aye. I'd planned to rob them from the start – and now their own fellows have done it for us. On our way back, we shall take our pick of the spoils.'

He rode on and reached the tavern. Yishana was waiting there, nervously, dressed for travelling.

When she saw Elric's face she sighed with satisfaction and smiled silkily. 'So Theleb K'aarna is dead,' she said. 'Good – how we can resume our interrupted relationship, Elric.'

The albino nodded. 'That was my part of the bargain – you kept yours when you helped Moonglum to get my sword back for me.' He was calm-faced – showing no emotion.

She embraced him, but he drew back. 'Later,' he murmured. 'But that is one promise I shall not break, Yishana.'

He helped the puzzled woman mount her waiting horse. They rode back towards Pilarmo's house.

She asked: 'And what of Nikorn – is he safe? I liked that man.'

'He died.' Elric's voice was strained.

'How?' she asked.

'Because, like all merchants,' Elric answered, 'he bargained too hard.'

There was an unnatural silence among the three as they made their horses speed faster towards the Gates of Bakshaan, and Elric did not stop when the others did, to take their pick of Pilarmo's riches. He rode on, unseeing, and the others had to spur their steeds in order to catch up with him, two miles beyond the city.

Over Bakshaan, no breeze stirred in the gardens of the rich. No winds came to blow cool on the sweating faces of the poor. Only the sun blazed in the heavens, round and red; and a shadow, shaped like a dragon, moved across it once, and then was gone.

Kings in Darkness

Three Kings in Darkness lie,
Gutheran of Org, and I,
Under a bleak and sunless sky –
The third Beneath the Hill.
          – Song of Veerkad

1

IT WAS Elric, Lord of the lost and sundered Empire of Melniboné, who rode like a fanged wolf from a trap – all slavering madness and mirth. He rode from Nadsokor, City of Beggars, and there was hate in his wake. The citizens had judged him rightly for what he was – a nigromancer of superlative powers. Now they hounded him and also the grotesque little man who rode laughing at Elric's side; Moonglum the Outlander, from Elwher and the unmapped East.

The flames of brands devoured the velvet of the night as the yelling, ragged throng pushed their bony nags in pursuit of the pair.

Starvelings and tattered jackals that they were, there was strength in their gaudy numbers and long knives and bone bows glinted in the brandlight. They were too strong for a couple of men to fight, too few to represent serious danger in a hunt, so Elric and Moonglum had chosen to leave the city without dispute and now sped towards the full and rising moon which stabbed its sickly beams through the darkness to show them the disturbing waters of the Varkalk River and a chance of escape from the incensed mob.

They had half a mind to stand and face the mob, since the Varkalk was their only alternative. But they knew well what the beggars would do to them, whereas they were uncertain what would become of them once they had entered the river. The horses reached the sloping banks of the Varkalk and reared, with hooves lashing.

Cursing, the two men spurred the steeds and forced them down towards the water. Into the river the horses plunged, snorting and spluttering. Into the river which led a roaring course towards the hell-spawned Forest of Troos which lay within the borders of Org, country of necromancy and rotting, ancient evil.

Elric blew water away from his mouth and coughed. 'They'll not follow us to Troos, I think!' he shouted at his companion.

Moonglum said nothing. He only grinned, showing his white teeth and the unhidden fear in his eyes. The horses swam strongly with the current and behind them the ragged mob shrieked in frustrated blood-lust while some of their number laughed and jeered.

'Let the forest do our work for us!'

Elric laughed back at them, wildly, as the horses swam on down the dark, straight river, wide and deep, towards a sun-starved morning, cold and spiky with ice. Scattered, slim-peaked crags loomed on either side of the flat plain, through which the river ran swiftly. Green-tinted masses of jutting blacks and browns spread colour through the rocks and the grass was waving on the plain as if for some purpose. Through the dawnlight, the beggar crew chased along the banks, but eventually gave up their quarry to return, shuddering, to Nadsokor.

When they had gone, Elric and Moonglum made their mounts swim towards the banks and climb them, stumbling, to the top where rocks and grass had already given way to sparse forest land which rose starkly on all sides, staining the earth with sombre shades. The foliage waved jerkily, as if alive – sentient.

It was a forest of malignantly erupting blooms, blood-coloured and sickly-mottled. A forest of bending, sinuously smooth trunks, black and shiny; a forest of spiked leaves of murky purples and gleaming greens – certainly an unhealthy place if judged only by the odour of rotting vegetation which was almost unbearable, impinging as it did upon the fastidious nostrils of Elric and Moonglum.

Moonglum wrinkled his nose and jerked his head in the direction they had come. 'Back now?' he inquired. 'We can avoid Troos and cut swiftly across a corner of Org to be in

Bakshaan in just over a day. What say you, Elric?'

Elric frowned. 'I don't doubt they'd welcome us in Bakshaan with the same warmth we received in Nadsokor. They'll not have forgotten the destruction we wrought there – and the wealth we acquired from their merchants. No, I have a fancy to explore the forest a little. I have heard tales of Org and its unnatural forest and should like to investigate the truth of them. My blade and sorcery will protect us, if necessary.'

Moonglum sighed. 'Elric – this once, let us not court the danger.'

Elric smiled icily. His scarlet eyes blazed out of his dead-white skin with peculiar intensity. 'Danger? It can bring only death.'

'Death is not to my liking, just yet,' Moonglum said. 'The fleshpots of Bakshaan, or if you prefer – Jadmar – on the other hand . . .'

But Elric was already urging his horse onward, heading for the forest. Moonglum sighed and followed.

Soon dark blossoms hid most of the sky, which was dark enough, and they could see only a little way in all directions. The rest of the forest seemed vast and sprawling; they could sense this, though sight of most of it was lost in the depressing gloom.

Moonglum recognised the forest from descriptions he had heard from mad-eyed travellers who drank purposefully in the shadows of Nadsokor's taverns.

'This is the Forest of Troos, sure enough,' he said to Elric. 'It's told of how the Doomed Folk released tremendous forces upon the earth and caused terrible changes among men, beasts and vegetation. This forest is the last they created, and the last to perish. They must have resented the planet giving them birth.'

'A child will always hate its parents at certain times,' Elric said impassively.

'Children of whom to be extremely wary, I should think,' Moonglum retorted. 'Some say that when they were at the peak of their power, they had no Gods to frighten them.'

'A daring people, indeed,' Elric replied, with a faint smile. 'They have my respect. But their lack of Gods and fear was probably our downfall, if not theirs. Now fear and the Gods are back and that, at least, is comforting.'

116

Moonglum puzzled over this for a short time, and then, eventually, said nothing.

He was beginning to feel uneasy.

The place was full of malicious rustlings and whispers, though no living animal inhabited it, as far as they could tell. There was a discomforting absence of birds, rodents or insects and, though they normally had no love for such creatures, they would have appreciated their company in the disconcerting forest.

In a quavering voice, Moonglum began to sing a song in the hope that it would keep his spirits up and his thoughts off the lurking forest.

'A grin and a word is my trade;
From these, my profit is made.
Though my body's not tall and my courage is small,
My fame will take longer to fade.'

So singing, with his natural amiability returning, Moonglum rode after the man he regarded as a friend – a friend who possessed something akin to mastery over him, though neither admitted it.

Elric smiled at Moonglum's song. 'To sing of one's own lack of size and absence of courage is not an action designed to ward off one's enemies, Moonglum.'

'But this way I offer no provocation,' Moonglum replied glibly. 'If I sing of my shortcomings, I am safe. If I were to boast of my talents, then someone might consider this to be a challenge and decide to teach me a lesson.'

'True,' Elric assented gravely, 'and well-spoken.'

He began pointing at certain blossoms and leaves, remarking upon their alien tint and texture, referring to them in words which Moonglum could not understand, though he knew the words to be part of a sorcerer's vocabulary. The albino seemed to be untroubled by the fears which beset the Eastlander, but often, Moonglum knew, appearances with Elric could hide the opposite of what they indicated.

They stopped for a short break while Elric sifted through some of the samples he had torn from trees and plants. He carefully placed his prizes in his belt-pouch but would say nothing of why he did so to Moonglum.

117

'Come,' he said, 'Troos's mysteries await us.'

But then a new voice, a woman's, said softly from the gloom: 'Save the excursion for another day, strangers.'

Elric reined his horse, one hand at *Stormbringer's* hilt. The voice had had an unusual effect upon him. It had been low, deep and had, for a moment, sent the pulse in his throat throbbing. Incredibly, he sensed that he was suddenly standing on one of Fate's roads, but where the road would take him, he did not know. Quickly, he controlled his mind and then his body and looked towards the shadows from where the voice had come.

'You are very kind to offer us advice, madam,' he said sternly. 'Come, show yourself and give explanation . . .'

She rode out then, very slowly, on a black-coated gelding that pranced with a power she could barely restrain. Moonglum drew an appreciative breath, for although heavy-featured, she was incredibly beautiful. Her face and bearing was patrician, her eyes were grey-green, combining enigma and innocence. She was very young. For all her obvious womanhood and beauty, Moonglum aged her at seventeen or little more.

Elric frowned: 'Do you ride alone?'

'I do now,' she replied, trying to hide her obvious astonishment at the albino's weird lack of colouring. 'I need aid – protection. Men who will escort me safely to Karlaak. There, they will be paid.'

'Karlaak, by the Weeping Waste? It lies the other side of Ilmiora, a hundred leagues away and a week's travelling at speed.' Elric did not wait for her to reply to this statement. 'We are not hirelings, madam. We are noblemen in our own lands.'

'Then you are bound by the vows of chivalry, sir, and cannot refuse my request.'

Elric laughed shortly. 'Chivalry, madam? We come not from the upstart nations of the South with their strange codes and rules of behaviour. We are nobles of older stock whose actions are governed by our own desires. You would not ask what you do, if you knew our names.'

She wetted her full lips with her tongue and said almost timidly: 'You are . . . ?'

'Elric of Melniboné, madam, called Elric Woman-slayer in the West, and this is Moonglum of Elwher; he has no conscience.'

She gasped. 'I have heard of you. There are stories – legends –

118

the white-faced reaver, the hell-driven sorcerer with a blade that drinks the souls of men . . .'

'Aye, that's true. And however magnified they are with the retelling, they cannot hint, those tales, at the darker truths which lie in their origin. Now, madam, do you still seek our aid?' Elric's voice was gentle, without menace, as he saw that she was very much afraid, although she had managed to control the signs of fear and her lips were tight with determination.

'I have no choice. I am at your mercy. My father, the Senior Senator of Karlaak, is very rich. Karlaak is called the City of the Jade Towers, as you will know, and such rare jades and ambers we have. Many could be yours.'

'Be careful, madam, lest you anger me,' warned Elric, although Moonglum's bright eyes lighted with avarice. 'We are not nags to be hired or goods to be bought. Besides which,' he smiled disdainfully, 'I am from crumbling Imrryr, the Dreaming City, from the Isle of the Dragon, hub of Ancient Melniboné, and I know what beauty really is. Your baubles cannot tempt one who has looked upon the milky Heart of Arioch, upon the blinding iridescence that throbs from the Ruby Throne, of the languorous and unnameable colours in the Actorios stone of the Ring of Kings. These are more than jewels, madam – they contain the life-stuff of the universe.'

'I apologise, Lord Elric, and to you Sir Moonglum.'

Elric laughed, almost with affection. 'We are grim clowns, lady, but the Gods of Luck, aided our escape from Nadsokor and we owe them a debt. We'll escort you to Karlaak, City of the Jade Towers, and explore the Forest of Troos another time.'

Her thanks was tempered with a wary look in her eyes.

'And now we have made introductions,' said Elric, 'perhaps you would be good enough to give your name and tell us your story.'

'I am Zarozinia from Karlaak, a daughter of the Voashoon, the most powerful clan in South Eastern Ilmiora. We have kinsmen in the trading cities on the coasts of Pikarayd and I went with two cousins and my uncle to visit them.'

'A perilous journey, Lady Zarozinia.'

'Aye and there are not only natural dangers, sir. Two weeks ago we made our goodbyes and began the journey home.

Safely we crossed the Straits of Vilmir and there employed men-at-arms, forming a strong caravan to journey through Vilmiro and so on to Ilmiora. We skirted Nadsokor since we had heard that the City of Beggars is inhospitable to honest travellers . . .'

Here, Elric smiled: 'And sometimes to dishonest travellers, as we can appreciate.'

Again the expression on her face showed that she had some difficulty in equating his obvious good humour with his evil reputation. 'Having skirted Nadsokor,' she continued, 'we came this way and reached the borders of Org wherein, of course, Troos lies. Very warily we travelled, knowing dark Org's reputation, along the fringes of the forest. And then we were ambushed and our hired men-at-arms deserted us.'

'Ambushed, eh?' broke in Moonglum. 'By whom, madam, did you know?"

'By their unsavoury looks and squat shapes they seemed native Orgians. They fell upon the caravan and my uncle and cousins fought bravely but were slain. One of my cousins slapped the rump of my gelding and sent it galloping so that I could not control it. I heard – terrible screams – mad, giggling shouts – and when I at last brought my horse to a halt, I was lost. Later I heard you approach and waited in fear for you to pass, thinking you also were Orgians, but when I heard your accents and some of your speech, I thought that you might help me.'

'And help you we shall, madam,' said Moonglum bowing gallantly from the saddle. 'And I am indebted to you for convincing Lord Elric here of your need. But for you, we should be deep in this awful forest by now and experiencing strange terrors no doubt. I offer my sorrow for your dead kinfolk and assure you that you will be protected from now onwards by more than swords and brave hearts, for sorcery can be called up if needs be.'

'Let's hope there'll be no need,' frowned Elric. 'You talk blithely of sorcery, friend Moonglum – you who hate me to use the art.'

Moonglum grinned.

'I was consoling the young lady, Elric. And I've had occasion to be grateful for your horrid powers, I'll admit. Now I suggest that we make camp for the night and so refreshed be on our

120

way at dawn.'

'I'll agree to that,' said Elric, glancing almost with embarrassment at the girl. Again he felt the pulse in his throat begin to throb and this time he had more difficulty in controlling it.

The girl also seemed fascinated by the albino. There was an attraction between them which might be strong enough to throw both their destinies along wildly different paths than any they had guessed.

Night came again quickly, for the days were short in those parts. While Moonglum tended the fire, nervously peering around him, Zarozinia, her richly embroidered cloth-of-gold gown shimmering in the firelight, walked gracefully to where Elric sat sorting the herbs he had collected. She glanced at him cautiously and then seeing that he was absorbed, stared at him with open curiosity.

He looked up and smiled faintly, his eyes for once unprotected, his strange face frank and pleasant. 'Some of these are healing herbs,' he said, 'and others are used in summoning spirits. Yet others give unnatural strength to the imbiber and some turn men mad. They will be useful to me.'

She sat down beside him, her thick-fingered hands pushing her black hair back. Her full breasts lifted and fell rapidly.

'Are you really the terrible evil-bringer of the legends, Lord Elric? I find it hard to credit.'

'I have brought evil to many places,' he said, 'but usually there has already been evil to match mine. I seek no excuses, for I know what I am and I know what I have done. I have slain malignant sorcerers and destroyed oppressors, but I have also been responsible for slaying fine men, and a woman, my cousin, whom I loved, I killed – or my sword did.'

'And you are master of your sword?'

'Yes – perhaps. I often wonder. Without it, I am helpless.' He put his hand around *Stormbringer's* hilt. 'I should be grateful to it.' Once again his red eyes seemed to become deeper, protecting some bitter emotion which was rooted at the core of his soul.

'I'm sorry if I revived unpleasant recollection . . . '

'Do not feel sorry, Lady Zarozinia. The pain is within me – you did not put it there. In fact I'd say you relieve it greatly by your presence.'

121

Half-startled, she glanced at him and smiled. 'I am no wanton, sir,' she said, 'but . . .'

He got up quickly.

'Moonglum, is the fire going well?'

'Aye, Elric. She'll stay in for the night.' Moonglum cocked his head on one side. It was unlike Elric to make such empty queries, but Elric said nothing further so the Eastlander shrugged, turned away to check his gear.

Since he could think of little else to say, Elric turned and said quietly, urgently: 'I'm a killer and a thief, not fit to . . .'

'Lord Elric, I am . . .'

'You are infatuated by a legend, that is all.'

'No! If you feel what I feel, then you'll know it's more.'

'You are young.'

'Old enough.'

'Beware. I must fulfil my destiny.'

'Your destiny?'

'It is no destiny at all, but an awful thing called doom. And I have no pity at all except when I see something in my own soul. Then I have pity – and I pity. But I hate to look and this is part of the doom which drives me. Not Fate, nor the Stars, nor Men, nor Demons, nor Gods. Look at me, Zarozinia – it is Elric, poor white chosen plaything of the Gods of Time – Elric of Melniboné who causes his own gradual and terrible destruction.'

'It is suicide!'

'Aye. Suicide of a dreadful sinning kind, for I drive myself to slow death. And those who go with me suffer also.'

'You speak falsely. Lord Elric – from guilt-madness.'

'Because I am guilty, lady.'

'And does Sir Moonglum go to doom with you?'

'He is unlike others – he is indestructible in his own self-assurance.'

'I am confident, also, Lord Elric.'

'But your confidence is that of youth, it is different.

'Need I lose it with my youth?'

'You have strength. You are as strong as we are. I'll grant you that.'

She opened her arms, rising. 'Then be reconciled, Elric of Melniboné.'

And he was. He seized her greedily, kissed her with a deeper need than that of passion. For the first time, Cymoril of Myrryr was forgotten as they dropped to the soft turf, oblivious of Moonglum who polished away at his curved sword with wry jealousy.

They all slept and the fire waned.

Elric, in his joy, had forgotten, or not heeded, that he had a watch to take and Moonglum, who had no source of strength but himself, stayed awake for as long as he could but sleep overcame him.

In the shadows of the awful trees, figures moved with shambling caution.

The misshapen men of Org began to creep inwards towards the sleepers.

Then Elric opened his eyes, aroused by instinct, stared at Zarozinia's peaceful face beside him, moved his eyes without turning his head and saw the danger. He rolled over, grasped *Stormbringer* and tugged the runeblade from his sheath. The sword hummed, as if in anger at being awakened.

'Moonglum!' Danger! Elric bellowed in fear, for he had more to protect than his own life. The little man's head jerked up. His curved sabre was already across his knees and he jumped to his feet, ran towards Elric as the Orgians closed in.

'I apologise,' he said.

'My fault, I . . . '

And then the Orgians were at them. Elric and Moonglum stood over the girl as she came awake, saw the situation and did not scream. Instead she looked around for a weapon but found none. She remained still, where she was, the only thing to do.

Smelling like offal, the gibbering Orgians, some dozen of them, slashed at Elric and Moonglum with heavy blades like cleavers, long and dangerous.

Stormbringer whined and smote through a cleaver, cut into an Orgian's neck and beheaded him. Blood gurgled from the corpse as it slumped back across the fire. Moonglum ducked beneath a howling cleaver, lost his balance, fell, slashed at his opponent's legs and hamstrung him so that he collapsed shrieking. Moonglum stayed on the ground and lunged upwards, taking another in the heart. Then he sprang to his feet and stood shoulder to shoulder with Elric while Zarozinia got up behind them.

'The horses,' grunted Elric. 'If it's safe, try to get them.'

There were still seven Orgians standing and Moonglum groaned as a cleaver sliced flesh from his left arm, retaliated, pierced the man's throat, turned slightly and sheared off another's face. They pressed forward, taking the attack to the incensed Orgians. His left hand covered with his own blood, Moonglum painfully pulled his long poignard from its sheath and held it with his thumb along the handle, blocked an opponent's swing, closed in and killed him with a ripping upward thrust of the dagger, the action of which caused his wound to pound with agony.

Elric held his great runesword in both hands and swung it in a semi-circle, hacking down the howling misshapen things. Zarozinia darted towards the horses, leaped on to her own and led the other two towards the fighting men. Elric smote at another and got into his saddle, thanking his own forethought to leave the equipment on the horses in case of danger. Moonglum quickly joined him and they thundered out of the clearing.

'The saddle-bags,' Moonglum called in greater agony than that created by his wound. 'We've left the saddlebags!'

'What of it? Don't press your luck, my friend.'

'But all our treasure's in them!'

Elric laughed, partly in relief, partly from real humour. 'We'll retrieve them, friend, never fear.'

'I know you, Elric. You've no value for the realities.'

But even Moonglum was laughing as they left the enraged Orgians behind them and slowed to a canter.

Elric reached and hugged Zarozinia. 'You have the courage of your noble clan in your veins,' he said.

'Thank you,' she replied, pleased with the compliment, 'but we cannot match such swordsmanship as that displayed by you and Moonglum. It was fantastic.'

'Thank the blade,' he said shortly.

'No. I will thank you. I think you place too much reliance upon that hell weapon, however powerful it is.'

'I need it.'

'For what?'

'For my own strength and, now, to give strength to you.'

'I'm no vampire,'. she smiled, 'and need no such fearful strength as that supplies.'

'Then be assured that I do,' he told her gravely. 'You would not love me if the blade did not give me what I need. I am like a spineless sea-thing without it.'

'I do not believe that, but will not dispute with you now.'

They rode for a while without speaking.

Later, they stopped, dismounted, and Zarozinia put herbs that Elric had given her upon Moonglum's wounded arm and began to bind it.

Elric was thinking deeply. The forest rustled with macabre, sensuous sounds. 'We're in the heart of Troos,' he said, 'and our intention to skirt the forest has been forestalled. I have it in mind to call on the King of Org and so round off our visit.'

Moonglum laughed. 'Shall we send our swords along first? And bind our own hands?' His pain was already eased by the herbs which were having quick effect.

'I mean it. We owe, all of us, much to the Orgians. They slew Zarozinia's uncle and cousins, they wounded you and they now have our treasure. We have many reasons for asking the King for recompense. Also, they seem stupid and should be easy to trick.'

'Aye. The King will pay us back for our lack of common-sense by tearing our limbs off.'

'I'm in earnest. I think we should go.'

'I'll agree that I'd like our wealth returned to us. But we cannot risk the lady's safety, Elric.'

'I am to be Elric's wife, Moonglum. Therefore if he visits the King of Org, I shall come too.'

Moonglum lifted an eyebrow. 'A quick courtship.'

'She speaks the truth, however. We shall all go to Org – and sorcery will protect us from the King's uncalled-for wrath.'

'And still you wish for death and vengeance, Elric,' shrugged Moonglum mounting. 'Well, it's all the same to me since your roads, whatever else, are profitable ones. You may be the Lord of Bad Luck by your own reckoning, but you bring good luck to me, I'll say that.'

'No more courting death,' smiled Elric, 'but we'll have some revenge, I hope.'

'Dawn will be with us soon,' Moonglum said. 'The Orgian citadel lies six hours ride from here by my working, south-south-east by the Ancient Star, if the map I memorised in Nadsokor was correct.'

'You have an instinct for direction that never fails, Moonglum. Every caravan should have such a man as you.'

'We base an entire philosophy on the stars in Elwher,' Moonglum replied. 'We regard them as the master plan for everything that happens on Earth. As they revolve around the planet they see all things, past, present and future. They are our Gods.'

'Predictable Gods, at least,' said Elric and they rode off towards Org with light hearts considering the enormity of their risk.

2

Little was known of the tiny kingdom of Org save that the Forest of Troos lay within its boundaries and to that, other nations felt, it was welcome. The people were unpleasant to look upon, for the most part, and their bodies were stunted and strangely altered. Legend had it that they were the descendants of the Doomed Folk who had wrought such destruction upon the Earth an entire Time Cycle before. Their rulers, it was said, were shaped like normal men in so far as their outward bodily appearance went, but their minds were warped more horribly than the limbs of their subjects.

The inhabitants were few and were generally scattered, ruled by their king from his citadel which was also called Org.

It was for this citadel that Elric and his companions rode, and, as they did so, Elric explained how he planned to protect them all from the Orgians.

In the forest he had found a particular leaf which, when used with certain invocations (which were harmless in that the invoker was in little danger of being harmed by the spirits he marshalled) would invest that person, and anyone else to whom he gave the drug distilled from the leaf, with temporary invulnerability.

The spell somehow reknitted the skin and flesh structure so that it could withstand any edge and almost any blow. Elric explained, in a rare garrulous mood, how the drug and spell combined to achieve the effect, but his archaisms and esoteric words meant little to the other two.

They stopped an hour's ride from where Moonglum expected to find the citadel so that Elric could prepare the drug and invoke the spell.

He worked swiftly over a small fire, using an alchemist's pestle and mortar, mixing the shredded leaf with a little water. As the brew bubbled on the fire, he drew peculiar runes on the ground, some of which were twisted into such alien forms that they seemed to disappear into a different dimension and re-appear beyond it.

> *'Bone and blood and flesh and sinew,*
> *Spell and spirit bind anew;*
> *Potent potion work the life charm,*
> *Keep its takers safe from harm.'*

So Elric chanted as a small pink cloud formed in the air over the fire, wavered, reformed into a spiral shape which curled downwards into the bowl. The brew spluttered and then was still. The albino sorcerer said: 'An old boyhood spell, so simple that I'd near forgotten it. The leaf for the potion grows only in Troos and therefore it is rarely possible to perform.'

The brew, which had been liquid, had now solidified and Elric broke it into small pellets. 'Too much,' he warned, 'taken at one time is poison, and yet the effect can last for several hours. Not always, though, but we must accept that small risk.' He handed both of them a pellet which they received dubiously. 'Swallow them just before we reach the citadel,' he told them, 'or in the event of the Orgians finding us first.'

Then they mounted and rode on again.

Some miles to the south-east of Troos, a blind man sang a grim song in his sleep and so woke himself . . .

They reached the brooding citadel of Org at dusk. Guttural, drooling voices shouted at them from the battlements of the square-cut ancient dwelling place of the Kings of Org. The thick rock oozed moisture and was corroded by lichen and

127

sickly, mottled moss. The only entrance large enough for a mounted man to pass through was reached by a path almost a foot deep in evil-smelling black mud.

'What's your business at the Royal Court of Gutheran the Mighty?'

They could not see who asked the question.

'We seek hospitality and an audience with your liege,' called Moonglum cheerfully, successfully hiding his nervousness. 'We bring important news to Org.'

A twisted face peered down from the battlements. 'Enter, strangers, and be welcome,' it said unwelcomingly.

The heavy wooden drawgate shifted upwards to allow them entrance and the horses pushed their way slowly through the mud and so into the courtyard of the citadel.

Overhead, the grey sky was a racing field of black tattered clouds which streamed towards the horizon as if to escape the horrid boundaries of Org and the disgusting Forest of Troos.

The courtyard was covered, though not so deeply, with the same foul mud as had impaired their progress to the citadel. It was full of heavy, unmoving shadow. On Elric's right, a flight of steps went up to an arched entrance which was hung, partially, with the same unhealthy lichen he had seen on the outer walls and, also, in the Forest of Troos.

Through this archway, brushing at the lichen with a pale, beringed hand, a tall man came and stood on the top step, regarding the visitors through heavy-lidded eyes. He was, in contrast to the other Orgians, handsome, with a massive, leonine head and long hair as white as Elric's; although the hair on the head of this great, solid man was somewhat dirty, tangled, unbrushed. He was dressed in a heavy jerkin of quilted, embossed leather, a yellow kilt which reached to his ankles and he carried a wide-bladed dagger, naked in his belt. He was older than Elric, aged between forty and fifty and his powerful if somewhat decadent face was seamed and pock-marked.

He stared at them in silence and did not welcome them; instead he signed to one of the battlement guards who caused the drawgate to be lowered. It came down with a crash, blocking off their way of escape.

'Kill the men and keep the woman,' said the massive man in a low monotone. Elric had heard dead men speak in that manner.

As planned, Elric and Moonglum stood either side of Zarozinia and remained where they were, arms folded.

Puzzled, shambling Orgians came warily at them, their loose trousers dragging in the mud, their hands hidden by the long shapeless sleeves of their filthy garments. They swung their cleavers. Elric felt a faint shock as the blade thudded on to his arm, but that was all. Moonglum's experience was similar.

The Orgians fell back, amazement and confusion on their bestial faces.

The tall man's eyes widened. He put one ring-covered hand to his thick lips, chewing at a nail.

'Our swords have no effect upon them, King! They do not cut and they do not bleed. What are these folk?'

Elric laughed theatrically. 'We are not common folk, little human, be assured. We are the messengers of the Gods and come to your King with a message from our great masters. Do not worry, we shall not harm you since we are in no danger of being harmed. Stand aside and make us welcome.'

Elric could see that King Gutheran was puzzled and not absolutely taken in by his words. Elric cursed to himself. He had measured the Orgian's intelligence by those he had seen. This king, mad or not, was much more intelligent, was going to be harder to deceive. He led the way up the steps towards glowering Gutheran.

'Greetings, King Gutheran. The Gods have, at last, returned to Org and wish you to know this.'

'Org has had no Gods to worship for an eternity,' said Gutheran hollowly, turning back into the citadel. 'Why should we accept them now?'

'You are impertinent, King.'

'And you are audacious. How do I know you come from the Gods?' He walked ahead of them, leading them through the low-roofed halls.

'You saw that the swords of your subjects had no effect upon us.'

'True. I'll take that incident as proof for the moment. I suppose there must be a banquet in your – honour – I shall order it. Be welcome, messengers.' His words were ungracious but it was virtually impossible to detect anything from Gutheran's tone, since the man's voice stayed at the same pitch.

Elric pushed his heavy riding cloak back from his shoulders and said lightly: 'We shall mention your kindness to our masters.'

The Court was a place of gloomy halls and false laughter and although Elric put many questions to Gutheran, the king would not answer them, or did so by means of ambiguous phrases which meant nothing. They were not given chambers wherein they could refresh themselves but instead stood about for several hours in the main hall of the citadel and Gutheran, while he was with them and not giving orders for the banquet, sat slumped on his throne and chewed at his nails, ignoring them.

'Pleasant hospitality,' whispered Moonglum.

'Elric – how long will the effects of the drug last?' Zarozinia had remained close to him. He put his arm around her shoulders. 'I do not know. Not much longer. But it has served its purpose. I doubt if they will try to attack us a second time. However, beware of other attempts, subtler ones, upon our lives.'

The main hall, which had a higher roof than the others and was completely surrounded by a gallery which ran around it well above the floor, fairly close to the roof, was chilly and un-warmed. No fires burned in the several hearths, which were open and let into the floor, and the walls dripped moisture and were undecorated; damp, solid stone, time-worn and gaunt. There were not even rushes upon the floor which was strewn with old bones and pieces of decaying food.

'Hardly house-proud, are they?' commented Moonglum looking around him with distaste and glancing at brooding Gutheran who was seemingly oblivious of their presence.

A servitor shambled into the hall and whispered a few words to the king. He nodded and arose, leaving the Great Hall.

Soon men came in, carrying benches and tables and began to place them about the hall.

The banquet was, at last, due to commence. And the air had menace in it.

The three visitors sat together on the right of the King who had donned a richly jewelled chain of kingship, whilst his son and several pale-faced female members of the Royal line sat on the left, unspeaking even among themselves.

Prince Hurd, a sullen-faced youth who seemed to bear a resentment against his father, picked at the unappetising food which was served them all.

He drank heavily of the wine which had little flavour but was strong, fiery stuff and this seemed to warm the company a little.

'And what do the Gods want of us poor Orgians?' Hurd said, staring hard at Zarozinia with more than friendly interest.

Elric answered: 'They ask nothing of you but your recognition. In return they will, on occasions, help you.'

'That is all?' Hurd laughed. 'That is more than those from the Hill can offer, eh, father?'

Gutheran turned his great head slowly to regard his son.

'Yes,' he murmured, and the word seemed to carry warning.

Moonglum said: 'The Hill – what is that?'

He got no reply. Instead a high-pitched laugh came from the entrance to the Great Hall. A thin, gaunt man stood there, staring ahead with a fixed gaze. His features, though emaciated, strongly resembled Gutheran's. He carried a stringed instrument and plucked at the gut so that it wailed and moaned with melancholy insistence.

Hurd said savagely: 'Look, father, 'tis blind Veerkad, the minstrel, your brother. Shall he sing for us?'

'Sing?'

'Shall he sing his songs, father?'

Gutheran's mouth trembled and twisted and he said after a moment: 'He may entertain our guests with an heroic ballad if he wishes, but . . . '

'But certain other songs he shall not sing . . . ' Hurd grinned maliciously. He seemed to be tormenting his father deliberately in some way which Elric could not guess. Hurd shouted at the blind man: 'Come Uncle Veerkad – sing!'

'There are strangers present,' said Veerkad hollowly above the wail of his own music. 'Strangers in Org?'

Hurd giggled and drank more wine. Gutheran scowled and continued to tremble, gnawing at his nails.

Elric called: 'We'd appreciate a song, minstrel.'

'Then you'll have the song of the Three Kings in Darkness, strangers, and hear the ghastly story of the Kings of Org.'

131

'No!' shouted Gutheran, leaping from his place, but Veerkad was already singing:

> *'Three Kings in darkness lie,*
> *Gutheran of Org, and I,*
> *Under a bleak and sunless sky –*
> *The third beneath the Hill.*
> *When shall the third arise?*
> *Only when another dies . . .'*

'Stop!' Gutheran got up in an obviously insane rage and stumbled across the table, trembling in terror, his face blanched, striking at the blind man, his brother. Two blows and the minstrel fell, slumping to the floor and not moving. 'Take him out! Do not let him enter again.' The king shrieked and foam flecked his lips.

Hurd, sober for a moment, jumped across the table, scattering dishes and cups and took his father's arm.

'Be calm, father. I have a new plan for our entertainment.'

'You! You seek my throne. 'Twas you who goaded Veerkad to sing his dreadful song. You know I cannot listen without . . .' He stared at the door. 'One day the legend shall be realised and the Hill-King shall come. Then shall I, you and Org perish.'

'Father,' Hurd was smiling horribly, 'let the female visitor dance for us a dance of the Gods.'

'What?'

'Let the woman dance for us, father.'

Elric heard him. By now the drug must have worn off. He could not afford to show his hand by offering his companions further doses. He got to his feet.

'What sacrilege do you speak, Prince?'

'We have given you entertainment. It is the custom in Org for our visitors to give us entertainment also.'

The hall was filled with menace. Elric regretted his plan to trick the Orgians, now. But there was nothing he could do. He had intended to exact tribute from them in the name of the Gods, but obviously these mad men feared more immediate and tangible dangers than any the Gods might represent.

He had made a mistake, put the lives of his friends in danger as well as his own. What should he do? Zarozinia murmured:

'I have learned dances in Ilmiora where all ladies are taught the art. Let me dance for them. It might placate them and bedazzle them to make our work easier.'

'Arioch knows our work is hard enough now. I was a fool to have conceived this plan. Very well, Zarozinia, dance for them, but with caution.' He shouted at Hurd: 'Our companion will dance for you, to show you the beauty that the Gods create. Then you must pay the tribute, for our masters grow impatient.'

'The tribute?' Gutheran looked up. 'You mentioned nothing of tribute.'

'Your recognition of the Gods must take the form of precious stones and metals, King Gutheran. I thought you to understand that.'

'You seem more like common thieves than uncommon messengers, my friends. We are poor in Org and have nothing to give away to charlatans.'

'Beware of your words, King!' Elric's clear voice echoed warningly through the hall.

'We'll see the dance and then judge the truth of what you've told us.'

Elric seated himself, grasped Zarozinia's hand beneath the table as she arose, giving her comfort.

She walked gracefully and confidently into the centre of the hall and there began to dance. Elric, who loved her, was amazed at her splendid grace and artistry. She danced the old, beautiful dances of Ilmiora, entrancing even the thick-skulled Orgians and, as she danced, a great golden Guest Cup was brought in.

Hurd leaned across his father and said to Elric: 'The Guest Cup, Lord. It is our custom that our guests drink from it in friendship.'

Elric nodded, annoyed at being disturbed in his watching of the wonderful dance, his eyes fixed on Zarozinia as she postured and glided. There was silence in the hall.

Hurd handed him the cup and absently he put it to his lips; seeing this Zarozinia danced on to the table and began to weave along it to where Elric sat. As he took the first sip, Zarozinia cried out and, with her foot, knocked the cup from his hand. The wine splashed on to Gutheran and Hurd who half rose, startled. 'It was drugged, Elric. They drugged it!'

Hurd lashed at her with his hand, striking her across the face. She fell from the table and lay moaning slightly on the filthy floor. 'Bitch! Would the messengers of the Gods be harmed by a little drugged wine?'

Enraged, Elric pushed aside Gutheran and struck savagely at Hurd so that the young man's mouth gushed blood. But the drug was already having effect. Gutheran shouted something and Moonglum drew his sabre, glancing upwards. Elric was swaying, his senses were jumbled and the scene had an unreal quality. He saw servants grasp Zarozinia but could not see how Moonglum was faring. He felt sick and dizzy, could hardly control his limbs.

Summoning up his last remaining strength, Elric clubbed Hurd down with one tremendous blow. Then he collapsed into unconsciousness.

3

There was the cold clutch of chains about his wrists and a thin drizzle was falling directly on to his face which stung where Hurd's nails had ripped it.

He looked about him. He was chained between two stone menhirs upon an obvious burial barrow of gigantic size. It was night and a pale moon hovered in the heavens above him. He looked down at the group of men below. Hurd and Gutheran were among them. They grinned at him mockingly.

'Farewell, messenger. You will serve us a good purpose and placate the Ones from the Hill!' Hurd called as he and the others scurried back towards the citadel which lay, silhouetted, a short distance away.

Where was he? What had happened to Zarozinia – and Moonglum? Why had he been chained thus upon – realisation and remembrance came – *the Hill!*

He shuddered, helpless in the strong chains which held him. Desperately he began to tug at them, but they would not yield. He searched his brain for a plan, but he was confused by torment and worry for his friends' safety. He heard a dreadful scuttling sound from below and saw a ghastly white shape dart into the gloom. Wildly he struggled in the rattling iron which held him.

In the Great Hall of the citadel, a riotous celebration was now reaching the state of an ecstatic orgy. Gutheran and Hurd were totally drunk, laughing insanely at their victory.

Outside the Hall, Veerkad listened and hated. Particularly he hated his brother, the man who had deposed and blinded him to prevent his study of sorcery by means of which he had planned to raise the King from Beneath the Hill.

'The time has come, at last,' he whispered to himself and stopped a passing servant.

'Tell me – where is the girl kept?'

'In Gutheran's chamber, master.'

Veerkad released the man and began to grope his way through the gloomy corridors up twisting steps, until he reached the room he sought. Here he produced a key, one of many he'd had made without Gutheran's knowing, and unlocked the door.

Zarozinia saw the blind man enter and could do nothing. She was gagged and bound with her own dress and still dazed from the blow Hurd had given her. They had told her of Elric's fate, but Moonglum had so far escaped them; guards hunted him now in the stinking corridors of Org.

'I've come to take you to your companion, lady,' smiled blind Veerkad, grasping her roughly with strength that his insanity had given him, picked her up and fumbled his way towards the door. He knew the passages of Org perfectly, for he had been born and grown up among them.

But two men were in the corridor outside Gutheran's chambers. One of them was Hurd, Prince of Org, who resented his father's appropriation of the girl and desired her for himself. He saw Veerkad bearing the girl away and stood silent while his uncle passed.

The other man was Moonglum, who observed what was happening from the shadows where he had hidden from the searching guards. As Hurd followed Veerkad, on cautious feet, Moonglum followed him.

Veerkad went out of the citadel by a small side door and carried his living burden towards the looming Burial Hill.

All about the foot of the monstrous barrow swarmed the leprous-white ghouls who sensed the presence of Elric, the Orgian's sacrifice to them.

Now Elric understood.

These were the things the Orgians feared more than the Gods. These were the living-dead ancestors of those who now revelled in the Great Hall. Perhaps these were actually the Doomed Folk. Was that their doom? Never to rest? Never to die? Just to degenerate into mindless ghouls? Elric shuddered.

Now desperation brought back his memory.

He cried to Arioch, the Demon God of Melniboné, and his voice was an agonised wail to the brooding sky and the pulsing earth.

'Arioch! Destroy the stones. Save your servant! Arioch – master – aid me!'

It was not enough. The ghouls gathered together and began to scuttle, gibbering up the barrow towards the helpless albino.

'Arioch! These are the things that would forsake your memory! Aid me to destroy them!'

The earth trembled and the sky became overcast, hiding the moon but not the white-faced, bloodless ghouls who were now almost upon him.

And then a ball of fire formed in the sky above him and the very sky seemed to shake and sway around it. Then, with a roaring crash two bolts of lightning slashed down, pulverising the stones and releasing Elric.

He got to his feet, knowing that Arioch would demand his price, as the first ghouls reached him.

He did not retreat, but in his rage and desperation leapt among them, smashing and flailing with the lengths of chain. The ghouls fell back and fled, gibbering in fear and anger, down the hill and into the barrow.

Elric could now see that there was a gaping entrance to the barrow below him; black against the blackness. Breathing heavily, he found that his belt pouch had been left him. From it he took a length of slim, gold wire and began frantically to pick at the locks of the manacles.

Veerkad chuckled to himself and Zarozinia hearing him was almost mad with terror. He kept drooling the words into her ear: 'When shall the third arise? Only when other dies. When that other's blood flows red – we'll hear the footfalls of the dead. You and I, we shall resurrect him and such vengeance will he wreak upon my cursed brother. Your blood, my dear, it will be that released him.' He felt that the ghouls were gone and judged them placated by their feast. 'Your lover has been useful to me,' he laughed as he began to enter the barrow. The smell of death almost overpowered the girl as the blind madman bore her downwards into the heart of the Hill.

Hurd, sobered after his walk in the colder air, was horrified when he saw where Veerkad was going; the barrow, the Hill of the King, was the most feared spot in the land of Org. Hurd paused before the black entrance and turned to run. Then, suddenly, he saw the form of Elric, looming huge and bloody, descending the barrow slope, cutting off his escape.

With a wild yell he fled into the Hill passage.

Elric had not previously noticed the Prince, but the yell startled him and he tried to see who had given it but was too late. He began to run down the steep incline towards the entrance of the barrow. Another figure came scampering out of the darkness.

'Elric! Thank the stars and all the Gods of Earth! You live!'

'Thank Arioch, Moonglum. Where's Zarozinia?'

'In there – the mad minstrel took her with him and Hurd followed. They are all insane, these kings and princes, I see no sense to their actions.'

'I have an idea that the minstrel means Zarozinia no good. Quickly, we must follow.'

'By the stars, the stench of death! I have breathed nothing like it – not even at the great battle of the Eshmire Valley where the armies of Elwher met those of Kaleg Vogun, usurper prince of the Tanghensi, and half a million corpses strewed the valley from end to end.'

'If you've no stomach . . . '

'I wish I had none. It would not be so bad. Come . . . '

They rushed into the passage, led by the far away sounds of Veerkad's maniacal laughter and the somewhat nearer movements of a fear-maddened Hurd who was now trapped between two enemies and yet more afraid of a third.

Hurd blundered along in the blackness, sobbing to himself in his terror.

In the weirdly phosphorescent Central Tomb, surrounded by the mummified corpses of his ancestors, Veerkad chanted the

137

resurrection ritual before the great coffin of the Hill-King – a giant thing, half as tall again as Veerkad who was tall enough. Veerkad was forgetful for his own safety and thinking only a vengeance upon his brother Gutheran. He held a long dagger over Zarozinia who lay huddled and terrified upon the ground near the coffin.

The spilling of Zarozinia's blood would be the culmination of the ritual and then –

Then Hell would, quite literally, be let loose. Or so Veerkad planned. He finished his chanting and raised the knife just as Hurd came screeching into the Central Tomb with his own sword drawn. Veerkad swung round, his blind face working in thwarted rage.

Savagely, without stopping for a moment, Hurd ran his sword into Veerkad's body, plunging the blade in up to the hilt so that its bloody point appeared sticking from his back. But the other, in his groaning death spasms, locked his hands about the Prince's throat. Locked them immovably.

Somehow, the two men retained a semblance of life and, struggling with each other in a macabre death-dance, swayed about the glowing chamber. The coffin of the Hill-King began to tremble and shake slightly, the movement hardly perceptible.

So Elric and Moonglum found Veerkad and Hurd. Seeing that both were near dead, Elric raced across the Central Tomb to where Zarozinia lay, unconscious, mercifully, from her ordeal. Elric picked her up and made to return.

He glanced at the throbbing coffin.

'Quickly, Moonglum. That blind fool has invoked the dead, I can tell. Hurry, my friend, before the hosts of Hell are upon us.'

Moonglum gasped and followed Elric as he ran back towards the cleaner air of night.

'Where to now, Elric?'

'We'll have to risk going back to the citadel. Our horses are there and our goods. We need the horses to take us quickly away, for I fear there's going to be a terrible blood-letting soon if my instinct is right.'

'There should not be too much opposition, Elric. They were all drunk when I left. That was how I managed to evade them so easily. By now, if they continued drinking as heavily as when

138

last I saw them, they'll be unable to move at all.'

'Then let's make haste.'

They left the Hill behind them and began to run towards the citadel.

4

Moonglum had spoken truth. Everyone was lying about the Great Hall in drunken sleep. Open fires had been lit in the hearths and they blazed, sending shadows skipping around the Hall. Elric said softly:

'Moonglum, go with Zarozinia to the stables and prepare our horses. I will settle our debt with Gutheran first.' He pointed. 'See, they have heaped their booty upon the table, gloating in their apparent victory.'

Stormbringer lay upon a pile of burst sacks and saddlebags which contained the loot stolen from Zarozinia's uncle and cousins and from Elric and Moonglum.

Zarozinia, now conscious but confused, left with Moonglum to locate the stables and Elric picked his way towards the table, across the sprawled shapes of drunken Orgians, around the blazing fires and caught up, thankfully, his hell-forged rune-blade.

Then he leaped over the table and was about to grasp Gutheran, who still had his fabulously gemmed chain of king-ship around his neck, when the great doors of the Hall crashed open and a howling blast of icy air sent the torches dancing and leaping. Elric turned, Gutheran forgotten, and his eyes widened.

Framed in the doorway stood the King from Beneath the Hill.

The long-dead monarch had been raised by Veerkad whose own blood had completed the work of resurrection. He stood in rotting robes, his fleshless bones covered by tight, tattered skin. His heart did not beat, for he had none; he drew no breath, for his lungs had been eaten by the creatures which feasted on such things. But, horribly, he lived . . .

The King from the Hill. He had been the last great ruler of the Doomed Folk who had, in their fury, destroyed half the Earth and created the Forest of Troos. Behind the dead King crowded

139

the ghastly hosts who had been buried with him in a legendary past.

The massacre began!

What secret vengeance was being reaped, Elric could only guess at – but whatever the reason, the danger was still very real.

Elric pulled out *Stormbringer* as the awakened horde vented their anger upon the living. The Hall became filled with the shrieking, horrified screams of the unfortunate Orgians. Elric remained, half-paralysed in his horror, beside the throne. Aroused, Gutheran woke up and saw the King from the Hill and his host. He screamed, almost thankfully:

'At last I can rest!'

And fell dying in a seizure, robbing Elric of his vengeance.

Veerkad's grim song echoed in Elric's memory. The Three Kings in Darkness – Gutheran, Veerkad and the King from Beneath the Hill. Now only the last lived – and he had been dead for millennia.

The King's cold, dead eyes roved the Hall and saw Gutheran sprawled upon his throne, the ancient chain of office still about his throat. Elric wrenched it off the body and backed away as the King from Beneath the Hill advanced. And then his back was against a pillar and there were feasting ghouls everywhere else.

The dead King came nearer and then, with a whistling moan which came from the depths of his decaying body, launched himself at Elric who found himself fighting desperately against the Hill-King's clawing, abnormal strength, cutting at flesh that neither bled nor suffered pain. Even the sorcerous rune-blade could do nothing against this horror that had no soul to take and no blood to let.

Frantically, Elric slashed and hacked at the Hill-King but ragged nails raked his flesh and teeth snapped at his throat. And above everything came the almost overpowering stench of death as the ghouls, packing the Great Hall with their horrible shapes, feasted on the living and the dead.

Then Elric heard Moonglum's voice calling and saw him upon the gallery which ran around the Hall. He held a great oil jar.

'Lure him close to the central fire, Elric. There may be a way to vanquish him. Quickly man, or you're finished!'

In a frantic burst of energy, the Melnibonéan forced the giant king towards the flames. Around them, the ghouls fed off the remains of their victims, some of whom still lived, their screams calling hopelessly over the sound of carnage.

The Hill-King now stood, unfeeling, with his back to the leaping central fire. He still slashed at Elric. Moonglum hurled the jar.

It shattered upon the stone hearth, spraying the King with blazing oil. He staggered, and Elric struck with his full power, the man and the blade combining to push the Hill-King backwards. Down went the King into the flames and the flames began to devour him.

A dreadful, lost howling came from the burning giant as he perished.

Flames licked everywhere throughout the Great Hall and soon the place was like Hell itself, an inferno of licking fire through which the ghouls ran about, still feasting, unaware of their destruction. The way to the door was blocked.

Elric stared around him and saw no way of escape – save one.

Sheathing *Stormbringer*, he ran a few paces and leaped upwards, just grasping the rail of the gallery as flames engulfed the spot where he had been standing.

Moonglum reached down and helped him to clamber across the rail.

'I'm disappointed, Elric,' he grinned, 'you forgot to bring the treasure.'

Elric showed him what he grasped in his left hand – the jewel-encrusted chain of kingship.

'This bauble is some reward for our hardship,' he smiled, holding up the glittering chain. 'I stole nothing, by Arioch! There are no kings left in Org to wear it! Come, let's join Zarozinia and get our horses.'

They ran from the gallery as masonry began to crash downwards into the Great Hall.

They rode fast away from the halls of Org and looking back saw great fissures appear in the walls and heard the roar of destruction as the flames consumed everything that had been Org. They had destroyed the seat of the monarchy, the remains of the Three Kings in Darkness, the present and the past.

141

Nothing would be left of Org save an empty burial mound and two corpses, locked together, lying where their ancestors had lain for centuries in the Central Tomb. They destroyed the last link with the previous Time Cycle and cleansed the Earth of an ancient evil. Only the dreadful Forest of Troos remained to mark the coming and the passing of the legendary Doomed Folk.

And the Forest of Troos was a warning.

Weary and yet relieved, the three saw the outlines of Troos in the distance, behind the blazing funeral pyre.

And yet, in his happiness, Elric had a fresh problem on his mind now that danger was past.

'Why do you frown now, love?' asked Zarozinia.

'Because I think you spoke the truth. Remember you said I placed too much reliance on my runeblade here?'

'Yes – and I said I would not dispute with you.'

'Agreed. But I have a feeling that you were partially right. On the burial mound and in it I did not have *Stormbringer* with me – and yet I fought and won, because I feared for your safety.' His voice was quiet. 'Perhaps, in time, I can keep my strength by means of certain herbs I found in Troos and dispense with the blade for ever?'

Moonglum shouted with laughter, hearing these words.

'Elric – I never thought I'd witness this. You daring to think of dispensing with that foul weapon of yours. I don't know if you ever shall, but the thought is comforting.'

'It is, my friend, it is.' He leaned in his saddle and grasped Zarozinia's shoulders, pulling her dangerously towards him as they galloped without slackening speed. And as they rode he kissed her, heedless of their pace.

'A new beginning!' he shouted above the wind. 'A new beginning, my love!'

And then they all rode laughing towards Karlaak by the Weeping Waste, to present themselves, to enrich themselves, and to attend the strangest wedding the Northern Lands had ever witnessed. For it would be more than a marriage between the awful evil-bringer of legends and a senator's youthful daughter – it would be a marriage between the dark wisdom of the Ancient World and the bright hope of the New.

And who could tell what such a combination would bring about?

The Earth would soon know, for Elric of Melniboné was the maker of legends and there were legends yet to make!

The Flame Bringers

1

BLOODY-BEAKED hawks soared on the frigid wind. They soared high above a mounted horde inexorably moving across the Weeping Waste.

The horde had crossed two deserts and three mountain ranges to be there and hunger drove them onwards. They were spurred on by remembrances of stories heard from travellers who had come to their Eastern homeland, by the encouragements of their thin-lipped leader who swaggered in his saddle ahead of them, one arm wrapped around a ten-foot lance decorated with the gory trophies of his pillaging campaigns.

The riders moved slowly and wearily, unaware that they were nearing their goal.

Far behind the horde, a stocky rider left Elwher, the singing, boisterous capital of the Eastern world, and came soon to a valley.

The hard skeletons of trees had a blighted look and the horse kicked earth the colour of ashes as its rider drove it fiercely through the sick wasteland that had once been gentle Eshmir, the golden garden of the East.

A plague had smitten Eshmir and the locust had stripped her of her beauty. Both plague and locust went by the same name – Terarn Gashtek, Lord of the Mounted Hordes, sunken-faced carrier of destruction; Terarn Gashtek, insane blood-drawer, the shrieking flame bringer. And that was his other name – Flame Bringer.

The rider who witnessed the evil that Terarn Gashtek had brought to gentle Eshmir was named Moonglum. Moonglum was riding, now, for Karlaak by the Weeping Waste, the last outpost of the Western civilisation of which those in the Eastlands knew little. In Karlaak, Moonglum knew he would find Elric of Melniboné who now dwelt permanently in his wife's graceful city. Moonglum was desperate to reach Karlaak quickly, to warn Elric and to solicit his help.

He was small and cocky, with a broad mouth and a shock of red hair, but now his mouth did not grin and his body was bent over the horse as he pushed it on towards Karlaak. For Eshmir, gentle Eshmir, had been Moonglum's home province and, with his ancestors, had formed him into what he was.

So, cursing, Moonglum rode for Karlaak.

But so did Terarn Gashtek. And already the Flame Bringer had reached the Weeping Waste. The horde moved slowly, for they had wagons with them which had at one time dropped far behind but now the supplies they carried were needed. As well as provisions, one of the wagons carried a bound prisoner who lay on his back cursing Terarn Gashtek and his slant-eyed battlemongers.

Drinij Bara was bound by more than strips of leather, that was why he cursed, for Drinij Bara was a sorcerer who could not normally be held in such a manner. If he had not succumbed to his weakness for wine and women just before the Flame Bringer had come down on the town in which he was staying, he would not have been trussed so, and Terarn Gashtek would not now have Drinij Bara's soul.

Drinij Bara's soul reposed in the body of a small, black cat – the cat which Terarn Gashtek had caught and carried with him always, for, as was the habit of Eastern sorcerers, Drinij Bara had hidden his soul in the body of the cat for protection. Because of this he was now slave to the Lord of the Mounted Hordes, and had to obey him lest the man slay the cat and so send his soul to Hell.

It was not a pleasant situation for the proud sorcerer, but he did not deserve less.

There was on the pale face of Elric of Melniboné some slight trace of an earlier haunting, but his mouth smiled and his crimson eyes were at peace as he looked down at the young, black-haired woman with whom he walked in the terraced gardens of Karlaak.

'Elric,' said Zarozinia, 'have you found your happiness?'

He nodded. 'I think so. That black runesword, *Stormbringer*, now hangs amid cobwebs in your father's armoury. The drugs I discovered in Troos keep me strong, my eyesight clear, and

145

need to be taken only occasionally. I need never think of travelling or fighting again. I am content, here, to spend my time with you and study the books in Karlaak's library. What more would I require?'

'You compliment me overmuch, my lord. I would become complacent.'

He laughed. 'Rather that than you were doubting. Do not fear, Zarozinia, I possess no reason, now, to journey on. Moonglum, I miss, but it was natural that he should become restless of residence in a city and wish to revisit his homeland.'

'I am glad you are at peace, Elric. My father was at first reluctant to let you live here, fearing the black evil that once accompanied you, but three months have proved to him that the evil has gone and left no fuming berserker behind it.'

Suddenly there came a shouting from below them, in the street a man's voice was raised and he banged at the gates of the house.

'Let me in, damn you, I must speak with your master.'

A servant came running: 'Lord Elric – there is a man at the gates with a message. He pretends friendship with you.'

'His name?'

'An alien one – Moonglum, he says.'

'Moonglum! His stay in Elwher has been short. Let him in!'

Zarozinia's eyes held a trace of fear and she held Elric's arm fiercely. 'Elric – pray he does not bring news to take you hence.'

'No news could do that. Fear not, Zarozinia.' He hurried out of the garden and into the courtyard of the house. Moonglum rode hurriedly through the gates, dismounting as he did so.

'Moonglum, my friend! Why the haste? Naturally, I am pleased to see you after such a short time, but you have been riding hastily – why?'

The little Eastlander's face was grim beneath its coating of dust and his clothes were filthy from hard riding.

'The Flame Bringer comes with sorcery to aid him,' he panted. 'You must warn the city.'

'The Flame Bringer? The name means nothing – you sound delirious, my friend.'

'Aye, that's true, I am. Delirious with hate. He destroyed my homeland, killed my family, my friends and now plans conquests in the West. Two years ago he was little more than an ordinary desert raider but then he began to gather a great horde of barbarians around him and has been looting and slaying his way across the Eastern lands. Only Elwher has not suffered from his attacks, for the city was too great for even him to take. But he has turned two thousand miles of pleasant country into a burning waste. He plans world conquest, rides westwards with five hundred thousand warriors!'

'You mentioned sorcery – what does this barbarian know of such sophisticated arts?'

'Little himself, but he has one of our greatest wizards in his power – Drinij Bara. The man was captured as he lay drunk between two wenches in a tavern. He had put his soul into the body of a cat so that no rival sorcerer might steal it while he slept. But Terarn Gashtek, the Flame Bringer, knew of this trick, seized the cat and bound its legs, eyes and mouth, so imprisoning Drinij Bara's evil soul. Now the sorcerer is his slave – if he does not obey the barbarian, the cat will be killed by an iron blade and Drinij Bara's soul will go to Hell.'

'These are unfamiliar sorceries to me,' said Elric. 'They seem little more than superstitions.'

'Who knows that they may be – but so long as Drinij Bara believes what he believes, he will do as Terarn Gashtek dictates. Several proud cities have been destroyed with the aid of his magic.'

'How far away is this Flame Bringer?'

'Three days' ride at most. I was forced to come hence by a longer route, to avoid his outriders.'

'Then we must prepare for a siege.'

'No, Elric – you must prepare to flee!'

'To flee – should I request the citizens of Karlaak to leave their beautiful city unprotected, to leave their homes?'

'If they will not – you must, and take your bride with you. None can stand against such a foe.'

'My own sorcery is no mean thing.'

'But one man's sorcery is not enough to hold back half a million men also aided by sorcery.'

'And Karlaak is a trading city – not a warriors' fortress. Very well, I will speak to the Council of Elders and try to convince them.'

'You must convince them quickly, Elric, for if you do not

147

Karlaak will not stand half a day before Terarn Gashtek's howling blood-letters.'

'They are stubborn,' said Elric as the two sat in his private study later that night. 'They refuse to realise the magnitude of the danger. They refuse to leave and I cannot leave them for they have welcomed me and made me a citizen of Karlaak.'

'Then we must stay here and die?'

'Perhaps. There seems to be no choice. But I have another plan. You say that this sorcerer is a prisoner of Terarn Gashtek. What would he do if he regained his soul?'

'Why he would take vengeance upon his captor. But Terarn Gashtek would not be so foolish as to give him the chance. There is no help for us there.'

'What if we managed to aid Drinij Bara?'

'How? It would be impossible.'

'It seems our only chance. Does this barbarian know of me or my history?'

'Not as far as I know.'

'Would he recognise you?'

'Why should he?'

'Then I suggest we join him.'

'Join him – Elric, you are no more sane than when we rode as free travellers together!'

'I know what I am doing. It would be the only way to get close to him and discover a subtle way to defeat him. We will set off at dawn, there is no time to waste.'

'Very well. Let's hope your old luck is good, but I doubt it now, for you've forsaken your old ways and the luck went with them.'

'Let us find out.'

'Will you take *Stormbringer*?'

'I had hoped never to have to make use of that hell-forged blade again. She's a treacherous sword at best.'

'Aye – but I think you'll need her in this business.'

'Yes, you're right. I'll take her.'

Elric frowned, his hands clenched. 'It will mean breaking my word to Zarozinia.'

'Better break it – than give her up to the Mounted Hordes.'

Elric unlocked the door to the armoury, a pitch torch flaring in one hand. He felt sick as he strode down the narrow passage lined with dulled weapons which had not been used for a century.

His heart pounded heavily as he came to another door and flung off the bar to enter the little room in which lay the disused regalia of Karlaak's long-dead War Chieftains – and *Stormbringer*. The black blade began to moan, as if welcoming him as he took a deep breath of the musty air and reached for the sword. He clutched the hilt and his body was racked by an unholy sensation of awful ecstasy. His face twisted as he sheathed the blade and he almost ran from the armoury towards cleaner air.

Elric and Moonglum mounted their plainly equipped horses and, garbed like common mercenaries, bade urgent farewell to the Councillors of Karlaak.

Zarozinia kissed Elric's pale hand.

'I realise the need for this,' she said, her eyes full of tears, 'but take care, my love.'

'I shall. And pray that we are successful in whatever we decide to do.'

'The White Gods be with you.'

'No – pray to the Demon Gods, to Arioch and Voroon – to the Lords of the Darks, for it is their evil help I'll need in this work. And forget not my words to the messenger who is to ride to the south-west and find Dyvim Slorm.'

'I'll not forget,' she said, 'though I worry lest you succumb again to your old black ways.'

'Fear for the moment – I'll worry about my own fate later.'

'Then farewell, my lord, and be lucky.'

'Farewell, Zarozinia. My love for you will give me more power even than this foul blade here.' He spurred his horse through the gates and then they were riding for the Weeping Waste and a troubled future.

2

Dwarfed by the vastness of the softly turfed plateau which was the Weeping Waste, the place of eternal rains, the

149

two horsemen drove their hard-pressed steeds through the drizzle.

A shivering desert warrior, huddled against the weather, saw them come towards him. He stared through the rain trying to make out details of the riders, then wheeled his stocky pony and rode swiftly back in the direction he had come. Within minutes he had reached a larger group of warriors attired like himself in furs and tasselled iron helmets. They carried short bone bows and quivers of long arrows fletched with hawk feathers. There were curved scimitars at their sides.

He exchanged a few words with his fellows and soon they were all lashing their horses towards the two riders.

'How much further lies the camp of Terarn Gashtek, Moonglum?' Elric's words were breathless, for both men had ridden for a day without halt.

'Not much farther, Elric. We should be – look!'

Moonglum pointed ahead. About ten riders came swiftly towards them. 'Desert barbarians – the Flame Bringer's men. Prepare for a fight – they won't waste time parleying.'

Stormbringer scraped from the scabbard and the heavy blade seemed to aid Elric's wrist as he raised it, so that it felt almost weightless.

Moonglum drew both his swords, holding the short one with the same hand with which he grasped his horse's reins.

The Eastern warriors spread out in a half circle as they rode down on the companions, yelling wild war-shouts. Elric reared his mount to a savage standstill and met the first rider with *Stormbringer's* point full in the man's throat. There was a stink like brimstone as it pierced flesh and the warrior drew a ghastly choking breath as he died, his eyes staring out in full realisation of his terrible fate – for *Stormbringer* drank souls as well as blood.

Elric cut savagely at another desertman, lopping off his sword arm and splitting his crested helmet and the skull beneath. Rain and sweat ran down his white, taut features and into his glowing crimson eyes, but he blinked it aside, half-fell in his saddle as he turned to defend himself against another howling scimitar, parried the sweep, slid his own runeblade down its length, turned the blade with a movement of his wrist and disarmed the warrior. Then he plunged his sword into the

150

man's heart and the desert warrior yelled like a wolf at the moon, a long baying shout before *Stormbringer* took his soul.

Elric's face was twisted in self-loathing as he fought intently with superhuman strength. Moonglum stayed clear of the albino's sword for he knew its liking for the lives of Elric's friends.

Soon only one opponent was left. Elric disarmed him and had to hold his own greedy sword back from the man's throat.

Reconciled to the horror of his death, the man said something in a guttural tongue which Elric half-recognised. He searched his memory and realised that it was a language close to one of the many ancient tongues which, as a sorcerer, he had been required to learn years before.

He said in the same language: 'Thou art one of the warriors of Terarn Gashtek the Flame Bringer.'

'That is true. And you must be the White-faced Evil One of legends. I beg you to slay me with a cleaner weapon than that which you hold.'

'I do not wish to kill thee at all. We were coming hence to join Terarn Gashtek. Take us to him.'

The man nodded hastily and clambered back on his horse.

'Who are you who speaks the High Tongue of our people?'

'I am called Elric of Melniboné – dost thou know the name?'

The warrior shook his head. 'No, but the High Tongue has not been spoken for generations, save by shamans – yet you're no shaman but, by your dress, seem a warrior.'

'We are both mercenaries. But speak no more. I will explain the rest to thy leader.'

They left a jackal's feast behind them and followed the quaking Easterner in the direction he led them.

Fairly soon, the low-lying smoke of many camp-fires could be observed and at length they saw the sprawling camp of the barbarian War Lord's mighty army.

The camp encompassed over a mile of the great plateau. The barbarians had erected skin tents on rounded frames and the camp had the aspect of a large primitive town. Roughly in the centre was a much larger construction, decorated with a motley assortment of gaudy silks and brocades.

Moonglum said, in the Western tongue: 'That must be Terarn Gashtek's dwelling. See, he has covered its half-cured

151

hides with a score of Eastern battle-flags.' His face grew grimmer as he noted the torn standard of Eshmir, the lion-flag of Okara and the blood-soaked pennants of sorrowing Changshai.

The captured warrior led them through the squatting ranks of barbarians who stared at them impassively and muttered to one another. Outside Terarn Gashtek's tasteless dwelling was his great war-lance decorated with more trophies of his conquests – the skulls and bones of Eastern princes and kings.

Elric said: 'Such a one as this must not be allowed to destroy the reborn civilisation of the Young Kingdoms.'

'Young kingdoms are resilient,' remarked Moonglum, 'but it is when they are old that they fall – and it is often Terarn Gashtek's kind that tear them down.'

'While I live he shall not destroy Karlaak – nor reach as far as Bakshaan.'

Moonglum said: 'Though, in my opinion, he'd be welcome to Nadsoker, the City of Beggars deserves such visitors as the Flame Bringer. If we fail, Elric, only the sea will stop him – and perhaps not that.'

'With Dyvim Slorm's aid – we shall stop him. Let us hope Karlaak's messenger finds my kinsman soon.'

'If he does not we shall be hard put to fight off half a million warriors, my friend.'

The barbarian shouted: 'Oh, Conqueror – mighty Flame Bringer – there are men here who wish to speak with you.'

A slurred voice snarled: 'Bring them in.'

They entered the badly smelling tent which was lighted by a fire flickering in a circle of stones. A gaunt man, carelessly dressed in bright captured clothing, lounged on a wooden bench. There were several women in the tent, one of whom poured wine into a heavy golden goblet which he held out.

Terarn Gashtek pushed the woman aside, knocking her sprawling and regarded the newcomers. His face was almost as fleshless as the skulls hanging outside his tent. His cheeks were sunken and his slanting eyes narrow beneath thick brows.

'Who are these?'

'Lord, I know not – but between them they slew ten of our men and would have slain me.'

'You deserved no more than death if you let yourself be

152

disarmed. Get out – and find a new sword quickly or I'll let the shamans have your vitals for divination.' The man slunk away.

Terarn Gashtek seated himself upon the bench once more.

'So, you slew ten of my bloodletters, did you, and came here to boast to me about it? What's the explanation?'

'We but defended ourselves against your warriors – we sought no quarrel with them.' Elric now spoke the cruder tongue as best he could.

'You defended yourselves fairly well, I grant you. We reckon three soft-living house-dwellers to one of us. You are a Westerner, I can tell that, though your silent friend has the face of an Elwherite. Have you come from the East or the West?'

'The West,' Elric said, 'we are free travelling warriors, hiring our swords to those who'll pay or promise us good booty.'

'Are all Western warriors as skilful as you?' Terarn Gashtek could not hide his sudden realisation that he might have underestimated the men he hoped to conquer.

'We are a little better than most,' lied Moonglum, 'but not greatly.'

'What of sorcery – is there much strong magic here?'

'No,' said Elric, 'the art has been lost to most.'

The barbarian's thin mouth twisted into a grin, half of relief, half of triumph. He nodded his head, reached into his gaudy silks and produced a small bound cat. He began to stroke its back. It wriggled but could do no more than glare at its captor. 'Then we need not worry,' he said.

'Now, why did you come here? I could have you tortured for days for what you did, slaying ten of my best outriders.'

'We recognised the chance of enriching ourselves by aiding you, Lord Flame Bringer,' said Elric. 'We could show you the richest towns, lead you to ill-defended cities that would take little time to fall. Will you enlist us?'

'I've need of such men as you, true enough. I'll enlist you readily – but mark this, I'll not trust you until you've proved loyal to me. Find yourselves quarters now – and come to the feast, tonight. There I'll be able to show you something of the power I hold – the power which will smash the strength of the West and lay it waste for ten thousand miles.'

'Thanks,' said Elric. 'I'll look forward to tonight.'

They left the tent and wandered through the haphazard

153

collection of tents and cooking fires, wagons and animals. There seemed little food, but wine was in abundance and the taut, hungry stomachs of the barbarians were placated with that.

They stopped a warrior and told him of Terarn Gashtek's orders to them. The warrior sullenly led them to a tent.

'Here – it was shared by three of the men you slew. It is yours by right of battle, as are the weapons and booty inside.'

'We're richer already,' grinned Elric with feigned delight.

In the privacy of the tent, which was less clean than Terarn Gashtek's, they debated.

'I feel uncommonly uncomfortable,' said Moonglum, 'surrounded by this treacherous horde. And every time I think of what they made of Eshmir, I itch to slay more of them. What now?'

'We can do nothing now – let us wait until tonight and see what develops.' Elric sighed. 'Our task seems impossible – I have never seen so great a horde as this.'

'They are invincible as they are,' said Moonglum. 'Even without Drinij Bara's sorcery to tumble down the walls of cities, no single nation could withstand them and, with the Western Nations squabbling among themselves, they could never unite in time. Civilisation itself is threatened. Let us pray for inspiration – your dark gods are at least sophisticated, Elric, and we must hope that they'll resent the barbarian's intrusion as much as we do.'

'They play strange games with their human pawns,' Elric replied, 'and who knows what they plan?'

Terarn Gashtek's smoke-wreathed tent had been further lighted by rush torches when Elric and Moonglum swaggered in, and the feast, consisting primarily of wine, was already in progress.

'Welcome, my friends,' shouted the Flame Bringer, waving his goblet. 'These are my captains – come, join them!'

Elric had never seen such an evil-looking group of barbarians. They were all half-drunk and, like their leader, had draped a variety of looted articles of clothing about themselves. But their swords were their own.

Room was made on one of the benches and they accepted

wine which they drank sparingly.

'Bring in our slave!' yelled Terarn Gashtek. 'Bring in Drinij Bara our pet sorcerer.' Before him on the table lay the bound and struggling cat and beside it an iron blade.

Grinning warriors dragged a morose-faced man close to the fire and forced him to kneel before the barbarian chief. He was a lean man and he glowered at Terarn Gashtek and the little cat. Then his eyes saw the iron blade and his gaze faltered.

'What do you want with me now?' he asked sullenly.

'Is that the way to address your master, spell-maker? Still, no matter. We have guests to entertain – men who have promised to lead us to fat merchant cities. We require you to do a few minor tricks for them.'

'I'm no petty conjurer. You cannot ask this of one of the greatest sorcerers in the world!'

'We do not ask – we order. Come, make the evening lively. What do you need for your magic-making? A few slaves – the blood of virgins? We shall arrange it.'

'I'm no mumbling shaman – I need no such trappings.'

Suddenly the sorcerer saw Elric. The albino felt the man's powerful mind tentatively probing his own. He had been recognised as a fellow sorcerer. Would Drinij Bara betray him?

Elric was tense, waiting to be denounced. He leaned back in his chair and, as he did so, made a sign with his hand which would be recognised by Western sorcerers – would the Easterner know it?

He did. For a moment he faltered, glancing at the barbarian leader. Then he turned away and began to make new passes in the air, muttering to himself.

The beholders gasped as a cloud of golden smoke formed near the roof and began to metamorphose into the shape of a great horse bearing a rider which all recognised as Terarn Gashtek. The barbarian leader leaned forward, glaring at the image.

'What's this?'

A map showing great land areas and seas seemed to unroll beneath the horse's hooves. 'The Western lands,' cried Drinij Bara. 'I make a prophecy.'

'What is it?'

The ghostly horse began to trample the map. It split and flew into a thousand smoky pieces. Then the image of the horseman faded, also, into fragments.

'Thus will the mighty Flame Bringer rend the bountiful nations of the West,' shouted Drinij Bara.

The barbarians cheered exultantly, but Elric smiled thinly. The Eastern wizard was mocking Terarn Gashtek and his men.

The smoke formed into a golden globe which seemed to blaze and vanish.

Terarn Gashtek laughed. 'A good trick, magic-maker – and a true prophecy. You have done your work well. Take him back to his kennel!'

As Drinij Bara was dragged away, he glanced questioningly at Elric but said nothing.

Later that night, as the barbarians drank themselves into a stupor, Elric and Moonglum slipped out of the tent and made their way to the place where Drinij Bara was imprisoned.

They reached the small hut and saw that a warrior stood guard at the entrance. Moonglum produced a skin of wine and, pretending drunkenness, staggered towards the man. Elric stayed where he was.

'What do you want, Outlander?' growled the guard.

'Nothing, my friend, we are trying to get back to our own tent, that's all. Do you know where it is?'

'How should I know?'

. .'True – how should you? Have some wine – it's good – from Terarn Gashtek's own supply.'

The man extended a hand. 'Let's have it.'

Moonglum took a swig of the wine. 'No, I've changed my mind. It's too good to waste on common warriors.'

'Is that so?' The warrior took several paces towards Moonglum. 'We'll find out, won't we? And maybe we'll mix some of your blood with it to give it flavour, my little friend.'

Moonglum backed away. The warrior followed.

Elric ran softly towards the tent and ducked into it to find Drinij Bara, wrists bound, lying on a pile of uncured hides. The sorcerer looked up.

'You – what do you want?'

'We've come to aid you, Drinij Bara.'

'Aid me? But why? You're no friend of mine. What would you gain? You risk too much.'

156

'As a fellow sorcerer, I thought I'd help you,' Elric said.

'I thought you were that. But, in my land, sorcerers are not so friendly to one another – the opposite, in fact.'

'I'll tell you the truth – we need your aid to halt the barbarian's bloody progress. We have a common enemy. If we can help you regain your soul, will you help?'

'Help – of course. All I do is plan the way I'll avenge myself. But for my sake be careful – if he suspects that you're here to aid me, he'll slay the cat and slay us, too.'

'We'll try to bring the cat to you. Will that be what you need?'

'Yes. We must exchange blood, the cat and I, and my soul will then pass back into my own body.'

'Very well, I'll try to –' Elric turned, hearing voices outside. 'What's that?'

The sorcerer replied fearfully, 'It must be Terarn Gashtek – he comes every night to taunt me.'

'Where's the guard?' The barbarian's harsh voice came closer as he entered the little tent. 'What's . . . ?' He saw Elric standing above the sorcerer.

His eyes were puzzled and wary. 'What are you doing here, Westerner – and what have you done with the guard?'

'Guard?' said Elric, 'I saw no guard. I was looking for my own tent and heard this cur cry out, so I entered. I was curious, anyway, to see such a great sorcerer clad in filthy rags and bound so.'

Terarn Gashtek scowled. 'Any more of such unwary curiosity my friend, and you'll be discovering what your own heart looks like. Now, get hence – we ride on in the morning.'

Elric pretended to flinch and stumbled hurriedly from the tent.

A lone man in the livery of an Official Messenger of Karlaak goaded his horse southwards. The mount galloped over the crest of a hill and the messenger saw a village ahead. Hurriedly he rode into it, shouting at the first man he saw.

'Quickly, tell me – know you aught of Dyvim Slorm and his Imrryrian mercenaries? Have they passed this way?'

'Aye – a week ago. They went towards Rignariom by Jadmar's border, to offer their services to the Vilmirian

Pretender.'

'Were they mounted or on foot?'

'Both.'

'Thanks, friend,' cried the messenger behind him and galloped out of the village in the direction of Rignariom.

The messenger from Karlaak rode through the night – rode along a recently made trail. A large force had passed that way. He prayed that it had been Dyvim Slorm and his Imrryrian warriors.

In the sweet-smelling garden city of Karlaak, the atmosphere was tense as the citizens waited for news they knew they could not expect for some time. They were relying on both Elric and on the messenger. If only one were successful, there would be no hope for them. Both had to be successful. Both.

3

The tumbling sound of moving men cut through the weeping morning and the hungry voice of Terarn Gashtek lashed at them to hurry.

Slaves packed up his tent and threw it into a wagon. He rode forward and wrenched his tall war-lance from the soft earth, wheeled his horse and rode westwards, his captains, Elric and Moonglum among them, behind him.

Speaking the Western tongue, Elric and Moonglum debated their problem. The barbarian was expecting them to lead him to his prey, his outriders were covering wide distances so that it would be impossible to lead him past a settlement. They were in a quandary for it would be disgraceful to sacrifice another township to give Karlaak a few days' grace, yet . . .

A little later two whooping outriders came galloping up to Terarn Gashtek.

'A town, lord! A small one and easy to take!'

'At last – this will do to test our blades and see how easy Western flesh is to pierce. Then we'll aim at a bigger target.' He turned to Elric: 'Do you know this town?'

'Where does it lie?' asked Elric thickly.

'A dozen miles to the south-west,' replied the outrider.

In spite of the fact that the town was doomed, Elric felt almost relieved. They spoke of the town of Gorjhan.

'I know it,' he said.

Cavim the Saddler, riding to deliver a new set of horse furniture to an outlying farm, saw the distant riders, their bright helmets caught by a sudden beam of sunlight. That the riders came from off the Weeping Waste was undoubtable – and he recognised menace in their massed progress.

He turned his mount about and rode with the speed of fear, back the way he had come to the town of Gorjhan.

The flat, hard mud of the street trembled beneath the thudding hooves of Cavim's horse and his high, excited shout knifed through shuttered windows.

'Raiders come!'Ware the raiders!'

Within a quarter of an hour, the head-men of the town had met in hasty conference and debated whether to run or to fight. The older men advised their neighbours to flee the raiders, other younger men preferred to stay ready, armed to meet a possible attack. Some argued that their town was too poor to attract any raider.

The townspeople of Gorjhan debated and quarrelled, and the first wave of raiders came screaming to their walls.

With the realisation that there was no time for further argument came the realisation of their doom, and they ran to the ramparts with their pitiful weapons.

Terarn Gashtek roared through the milling barbarians who churned the mud around Gorjhan: 'Let's waste no time in siege. Fetch the sorcerer!'

They dragged Drinij Bara forward. From his garments, Terarn Gashtek produced the small black cat and held an iron blade at its throat.

'Work your spell, sorcerer, and tumble the walls quickly.'

The sorcerer scowled, his eyes seeking Elric, but the albino averted his own eyes and turned his horse away.

The sorcerer produced a handful of powder from his belt pouch and hurled it into the air where it became first a gas, then a flickering ball of flame and finally a face, a dreadful unhuman face, formed in the flame.

'Dag-Gadden the Destroyer,' intoned Drinij Bara, 'you are sworn to our ancient pact – will you obey me?'

'I must, therefore I will. What do you command?'

'That you obliterate the walls of this town and so leave the men inside naked, like crabs without their shells.'

'My pleasure is to destroy and destroy I shall.' The flaming face faded, altered, shrieked a searing course upward and became a blossoming scarlet canopy which hid the sky.

Then it swept down over the town and, in the instant of its passing, the walls of Gorjhan groaned, crumbled and vanished.

Elric shuddered – if Dag-Gadden came to Karlaak, such would be their fate.

Triumphant, the barbarian battlemongers swept into the defenceless town.

Careful to take no part in the massacre, Elric and Moonglum were also helpless to aid the slaughtered townspeople. The sight of the senseless, savage bloodshed around them enervated them. They ducked into a small house which seemed so far untouched by the pillaging barbarians. Inside they found three cowering children huddled around an older girl who clutched an old scythe in her soft hands. Shaking with fear, she prepared to stand them off.

'Do not waste our time, girl,' Elric said, 'or you'll be wasting your lives. Does this house have a loft?'

She nodded.

'Then get to it quickly. We'll make sure you're unharmed.'

They stayed in the house, hating to observe the slaughter-madness which had come upon the howling barbarians. They heard the dreadful sounds of carnage and smelled the stench of dead flesh and running blood.

A barbarian, covered in blood which was not his own, dragged a woman into the house by her hair. She made no attempt to resist, her face stunned by the horror she had witnessed.

Elric growled: 'Find another nest, hawk – we've made this our own.'

The man said: 'There's room enough here for what I want.'

Then, at last, Elric's clenched muscles reacted almost in spite of him. His right hand swung over to his left hip and the long fingers locked around *Stormbringer's* black hilt. The blade leapt from the scabbard as Elric stepped forward and, his crimson eyes blazing his sickened hatred, he smashed his sword down through the man's body. Unnecessarily, he clove again, hacking the barbarian in two. The woman remained where she lay, conscious but unmoving.

Elric picked up her inert body and passed it gently to Moonglum. 'Take her upstairs with the others,' he said brusquely.

The barbarians had begun to fire part of the town, their slaying all but done. Now they looted. Elric stepped out of the doorway.

There was precious little for them to loot but, still hungry for violence, they spent their energy on smashing inanimate things and setting fire to the broken, pillaged dwellings.

Stormbringer dangled loosely in Elric's hand as he looked at the blazing town. His face was a mask of shadow and frisking light as the fire threw up still longer tongues of flame to the misty sky.

Around him, barbarians squabbled over the pitiful booty; and occasionally a woman's scream cut above the other sounds, intermingled with rough shouts and the clash of metal.

Then he heard voices which were pitched differently to those in the immediate vicinity. The accents of the reavers mingled with a new tone – a whining, pleading tone. A group led by Terarn Gashtek came into view through the smoke.

Terarn Gashtek held something bloody in his hand – a human hand, severed at the wrist – and behind him swaggered several of his captains holding a naked old man between them. Blood ran over his body and gushed from his ruined arm, spurting sluggishly.

Terarn Gashtek frowned when he saw Elric. Then he shouted: 'Now Westerner, you shall see how we placate our Gods with better gifts than meal and sour milk as this swine once did. He'll soon be dancing a pretty measure, I'll warrant – won't you, Lord Priest?'

The whining note went out of the old man's voice then and he stared with fever-bright eyes at Elric. His voice rose to a frenzied and high-pitched shriek which was curiously repellent.

'You dogs can howl over me!' he spat, 'but Mirath and T'aargano will be revenged for the ruin of their priest and their temple – you have brought flame here and you shall die by flame.' He pointed the bleeding stump of his arm at Elric – 'And you – you are a traitor and have been one in many causes, I can see it written in you. Though now . . . You are – ' the priest drew breath.

Elric licked his lips.

'I am what I am,' he said. 'And you are nothing but an old man soon to die. Your gods cannot harm us, for we do not pay them any respect. I'll listen no more to your senile meanderings!'

There was in the old priest's face all the knowledge of his past torment and the torment which was to come. He seemed to consider this and then was silent.

'Save your breath for screaming,' said Terarn Gashtek to the uncomprehending priest.

And then Elric said: 'It's bad luck to kill a priest, Flame Bringer!'

'You seem weak of stomach, my friend. His sacrifice to our own gods will bring us good luck, fear not.'

Elric turned away. As he entered the house again, a wild shriek of agony seared out of the night and the laughter which followed was not pleasant.

Later, as the still burning houses lit the night, Elric and Moonglum, carrying heavy sacks on their shoulders, clasping a woman each, moved with a simulation of drunkenness to the edge of the camp. Moonglum left the sacks and the women with Elric and went back, returning soon with three horses.

They opened the sacks to allow the children to climb out and watched the silent women mount the horses, aiding the children to clamber up.

Then they galloped away.

'Now,' said Elric savagely, 'we must work our plan tonight, whether the messenger reached Dyvim Slorm or not. I could not bear to witness another such sword-quenching.'

Terarn Gashtek had drunk himself insensible. He lay sprawled in an upper room of one of the unburned houses.

Elric and Moonglum crept towards him. While Elric watched to see that he was undisturbed, Moonglum knelt beside the barbarian leader and, light-fingered, cautiously reached inside the man's garments. He smiled in self-approval as he lifted out the squirming cat and replaced it with a stuffed rabbit-skin he had earlier prepared for the purpose. Holding the animal tight, he arose and nodded to Elric. Together, warily, they left the house and made their way through the chaos of the camp.

'I ascertained that Drinij Bara lies in the large wagon,' Elric told his friend. 'Quickly, now, the main danger's over.'

Moonglum said: 'When the cat and Drinij Bara have exchanged blood and the sorcerer's soul is back in his body – what then, Elric?'

'Together, our powers may serve at least to hold the barbarians back, but – ' he broke off as a large group of warriors came weaving towards them.

'It's the Westerner and his little friend,' laughed one. 'Where are you off to, comrades?'

Elric sensed their mood. The slaughter of the day had not completely satiated their blood-lust. They were looking for trouble.

'Nowhere in particular,' he replied. The barbarians lurched around them, encircling them.

'We've heard much of your straight blade, stranger,' grinned their spokesman, 'and I'd a mind to test it against a real weapon.' He grabbed his own scimitar out of his belt. 'What do you say?'

'I'd spare you that,' said Elric coolly.

'You are generous – but I'd rather you accepted my invitation.'

'Let us pass,' said Moonglum.

The barbarians' faces hardened. 'Speak you so to the conquerors of the world?' said the leader.

Moonglum took a step back and drew his sword, the cat squirming in his left hand.

'We'd best get this done,' said Elric to his friend. He tugged his runeblade from its scabbard. The sword sang a soft and mocking tune and the barbarians heard it. They were disconcerted.

'Well?' said Elric, holding the half-sentient blade out.

The barbarian who had challenged him looked uncertain of what to do. Then he forced himself to shout: 'Clean iron can withstand any sorcery,' and launched himself forward.

Elric, grateful for the chance to take further vengeance, blocked his swing, forced the scimitar back and aimed a blow which sliced the man's torso just above the hip. The barbarian screamed and died. Moonglum, dealing with a couple more, killed one but another came in swiftly and his sweeping sword sliced the little Eastlander's left shoulder. He howled – and dropped the cat. Elric stepped in, slew Moonglum's opponent, *Stormbringer* wailing a triumphant dirge. The rest of the barbarians turned and ran off.

'How bad is your wound?' gasped Elric, but Moonglum was on his knees staring through the gloom.

'Quick, Elric – can you see the cat? I dropped it in the struggle. If we lose it – we too are lost.'

Frantically, they began to hunt through the camp.

But they were unsuccessful, for the cat, with the dexterity of its kind, had hidden itself.

A few moments later they heard the sounds of uproar coming from the house which Terarn Gashtek had commandeered.

'He's discovered that the cat's been stolen!' exclaimed Moonglum. 'What do we do now?'

'I don't know – keep searching and hope he does not suspect us.'

They continued to hunt, but with no result. While they searched, several barbarians came up to them. One of them said:

'Our leader wishes to speak with you.'

'Why?'

'He'll inform you of that. Come on.'

Reluctantly, they went with the barbarians to be confronted by a raging Terarn Gashtek. He clutched the stuffed rabbit skin in one claw-like hand and his face was warped with fury.

'My hold over the sorcerer has been stolen from me,' he roared. 'What do you know of it?'

'I don't understand,' said Elric.

'The cat is missing – I found this rag in its place. You were caught talking to Drinij Bara recently, I think you were responsible.'

'We know nothing of this,' said Moonglum.

Terarn Gashtek growled: 'The camp's in disorder, it will take a day to re-organise my men – once loosed like this they will obey no one. But when I've restored order, I shall question the whole camp. If you tell the truth, then you will be released, but meanwhile you will be given all the time you need to speak with the sorcerer.' He jerked his head. 'Take them away, disarm them, bind them and throw them in Drinij Bara's kennel.'

As they were led away, Elric muttered: 'We must escape and find that cat, but meanwhile we need not waste this opportunity to confer with Drinij Bara.'

Drinij Bara said in the darkness: 'No, Brother Sorcerer, I will not aid you. I will risk nothing until the cat and I are united.'

'But Terarn Gashtek cannot threaten you any more.'

'What if he recaptures the cat – what then?'

Elric was silent. He shifted his bound body uncomfortably on the hard boards of the wagon. He was about to continue his attempts at persuasion when the awning was thrown aside and he saw another trussed figure thrown towards them. Through the blackness he said in the Eastern tongue: 'Who are you?'

The man replied in the language of the West: 'I do not understand you.'

'Are you, then, a Westerner?' asked Elric in the common speech.

'Yes – I am an Official Messenger from Karlaak. I was captured by these odorous jackals as I returned to the city.'

'What? Are you the man we sent to Dyvim Slorm, my kinsman? I am Elric of Melniboné.'

'My lord, are we all, then prisoners? Oh, gods – Karlaak is truly lost.'

'Did you get to Dyvim Slorm?'

'Aye – I caught up with him and his band. Luckily they were nearer to Karlaak than we suspected.'

'And what was his answer to my request?'

'He said that a few young ones might be ready, but even with sorcery to aid him it would take some time to get to the Dragon Isle. There is a chance.'

'A chance is all we need – but it will be no good unless we accomplish the rest of our plan. Somehow Drinij Bara's soul must be regained so that Terarn Gashtek cannot force him to defend the barbarians. There is one idea I have – a memory of an ancient kinship that we of Melniboné had for a being called Meerclar. Thank the gods that I discovered those drugs in Troos and I still have my strength. Now, I must call my sword to me.'

165

He closed his eyes and allowed his mind and body first to relax completely and then concentrate on one single thing – the sword *Stormbringer*.

For years the evil symbiosis had existed between man and sword and the old attachments lingered.

He cried: '*Stormbringer*! Sister *Stormbringer*, unite with your brother! Come, sweet runeblade, come hell-forged kinslayer, your master needs thee . . .'

Outside, it seemed that a wailing wind had suddenly sprung up. Elric heard shouts of fear and a whistling sound. Then the covering of the wagon was sliced apart to let in the starlight and the moaning blade quivered in the air over his head. He struggled upwards, already feeling nauseated at what he was about to do, but he was reconciled that he was not, this time, guided by self-interest but by the necessity to save the world from the barbarian menace.

'Give me thy strength, sister my sword,' he groaned as his bound hands grasped the hilt. 'Give me thy strength and let us hope it is for the last time.'

The blade writhed in his hands and he felt an awful sensation as its power, the power stolen vampire-like, from a hundred brave men, flowed into his shuddering body.

He became possessed of a peculiar strength which was not by any means wholly physical. His white face twisted as he concentrated on controlling the new power and the blade, both of which threatened to possess him entirely. He snapped his bonds and stood up.

Barbarians were even now running towards the wagon. Swiftly he cut the leather ropes binding the others and, unconscious of the nearing warriors, called a different name.

He spoke a new tongue, an alien tongue which normally he could not remember. It was a language taught to the Sorcerer Kings of Melniboné, Elric's ancestors, even before the building of Imrryr, the Dreaming City, over ten thousand years previously.

'Meerclar of the Cats, it is I, your kinsman, Elric of Melniboné, last of the line that made vows of friendship with you and your people. Do you hear me, Lord of the Cats?'

Far beyond the Earth, dwelling within a world set apart from

the physical laws of space and time which governed the planet,
glowing in a deep warmth of blue and amber, a manlike creature
stretched itself and yawned, displaying tiny, pointed teeth. It
pressed its head languidly against its furry shoulder – and listened.

The voice it heard was not that of one of its people, the kind
he loved and protected. But he recognised the language.

He smiled to himself as remembrance came and he felt the
pleasant sensation of fellowship. He remembered a race which,
unlike other humans (whom he disdained) had shared his qualities
– a race which, like him, loved pleasure, cruelty and sophistication
for its own sake. The race of Melnibonéans.

Meerclar, Lord of the Cats, Protector of the Feline Kind,
projected himself gracefully towards the source of the voice.

'*How may I aid thee?*' he purred.

'We seek one of your folk, Meerclar, who is somewhere close
to here.'

'*Yes, I sense him. What do you want of him?*'

'Nothing which is his – but he has two souls, one of them not
his own.'

'*That is so – his name is Fiarshern of the great family of*
Trrechoww. I will call him. He will come to me.'

Outside, the barbarians were striving to conquer their fear
of the supernatural events taking place in the wagon. Terarn
Gashtek cursed them: 'There are five hundred thousand of us
and a few of them. Take them now!'

His warriors began to move cautiously forward.

Fiarshern, the cat, heard a voice which it knew instinctively
to be that of one which it would be foolish to disobey. It ran
swiftly towards the source of that voice.

'Look – the cat – here it is. Sieze it quickly.'

Two of Terarn Gashtek's men jumped forward to do his
bidding, but the little cat eluded them and leaped lightly into
the wagon.

'*Give the human back its soul, Fiarshern,*' said Meerclar
softly. The cat moved towards its human master and dug its
delicate teeth into the sorcerer's veins.

A moment later Drinij Bara laughed wildly. 'My soul is mine
again. Thank you, great Cat Lord. Let me repay you!'

'*There is no need,*' smiled Meerclar mockingly, '*and, anyway,*
I perceive that your soul is already bartered. Goodbye, Elric of

Melniboné. I was pleased to answer your call, though I see that you no longer follow the ancient pursuits of your fathers. Still, for the sake of old loyalties I do not begrudge you this service. Farewell, I go back to a warmer place than this inhospitable one.'

The Lord of the Cats faded and returned to the world of blue and amber warmth where he once more resumed his interrupted sleep.

'Come, Brother Sorcerer,' cried Drinij Bara exultantly. 'Let us take the vengeance which is ours.'

He and Elric sprang from the wagon, but the two others were not quite so quick to respond.

Terarn Gashtek and his men confronted them. Many had bows and long arrows fitted to them.

'Shoot them down swiftly,' yelled the Flame Bringer. 'Shoot them now before they have time to summon further demons!'

A shower of arrows whistled towards them. Drinij Bara smiled, spoke a few words as he moved his hands almost carelessly. The arrows stopped in midflight, turned back and each uncannily found the throat of the man who had shot it. Terarn Gashtek gasped and wheeled back, pushing past his men and, as he retreated, shouted for them to attack the four.

Driven by the knowledge that if they fled they would be doomed, the great mass of barbarians closed in.

Dawn was bringing light to the cloud-ripped sky as Moonglum looked upwards. 'Look, Elric,' he shouted pointing.

'Only five,' said the albino. 'Only five – but perhaps enough.'

He parried several lashing blades on his own sword and, although he was possessed of superhuman strength, all the power seemed to have left the sword so that it was only as useful as an ordinary blade. Still fighting, he relaxed his body and felt the power leave him, flowing back into *Stormbringer*.

Again the runeblade began to whine and thirstily sought the throats and hearts of the savage barbarians.

Drinij Bara had no sword, but he did not need one, he was using subtler means to defend himself. All around him were the gruesome results, boneless masses of flesh and sinew.

The two sorcerers and Moonglum and the messenger forced their way through the half-insane barbarians who were desperately attempting to overcome them. In the confusion it was impossible to work out a coherent plan of action. Moonglum and the messenger grabbed scimitars from the corpses of the barbarians and joined in the battle.

Eventually, they had reached the outer limits of the camp. A whole mass of barbarians had fled, spurring their mounts westwards. Then Elric saw Terarn Gashtek, holding a bow. He saw the Flame Bringer's intention and shouted a warning to his fellow sorcerer who had his back to the barbarian. Drinij Bara, yelling some disturbing incantation, half-turned, broke off, attempted to begin another spell, but the arrow pierced his eye.

He screamed: '*No!*'

Then he died.

Seeing his ally slain, Elric paused and stared at the sky and the great wheeling beasts which he recognised.

Dyvim Slorm, son of Elric's cousin Dyvim Tvar the Dragon Master, had brought the legendary dragons of Imrryr to aid his kinsman. But most of the huge beasts slept, and would sleep for another century – only five dragons had been aroused. As yet, Dyvim Slorm could do nothing for fear of harming Elric and his comrades.

Terarn Gashtek, too, had seen the magnificent beasts. His grandiose plans of conquest were already fading and, thwarted, he ran towards Elric.

'You white-faced filth,' he howled, 'you have been responsible for all this – and you will pay the Flame Bringer's price!'

Elric laughed as he brought up *Stormbringer* to protect himself from the incensed barbarian. He pointed to the sky: 'These, too, can be called Flame Bringers, Terarn Gashtek – and are better named than thou!'

Then he plunged the evil blade full into Terarn Gashtek's body and the barbarian gave a choking moan as his soul was drawn from him.

'Destroyer, I may be, Elric of Melniboné,' he gasped, 'but my way was cleaner than yours. May you and all you hold dear be cursed for eternity!'

Elric laughed, but his voice shook slightly as he stared at the barbarian's corpse. 'I've rid myself of such curses once before, my friend. Yours will have little effect, I think.' He paused. 'By Arioch, I hope I'm right. I'd thought my fate cleansed of doom and curses, but perhaps I was wrong . . .'

The huge horde of barbarians were nearly all mounted now and fleeing westwards. They had to be stopped for, at the pace they were travelling, they would soon reach Karlaak and only the Gods knew what they would do when they got to the unprotected city.

Above him, he heard the flapping of thirty-foot wings and scented the familiar smell of the great flying reptiles which had pursued him years before when he had led a reaver fleet on the attack of his home-city. Then he heard the curious notes of the Dragon Horn and saw that Dyvim Slorm was seated on the back of the leading beast, a long spearlike goad in his gauntleted right hand.

The dragon spiralled downward and its great bulk came to rest on the ground thirty feet away, its leathery wings folding back along its length. The Dragon Master waved to Elric.

'Greetings, King Elric, we barely managed to arrive in time I see.'

'Time enough, kinsman,' smiled Elric. 'It is good to see the son of Dyvim Tvar again. I was afraid you might not answer my plea.'

'Old scores were forgotten at the Battle of Bakshaan when my father Dyvim Tvar died aiding you in the siege of Nikorn's fortress. I regret only the younger beasts were ready to be awakened. You'll remember the others were used but a few years past.'

'I remember,' said Elric. 'But may I beg another favour, Dyvim Slorm?'

'What is that?'

'Let me ride the chief dragon. I am trained in the arts of the Dragon Master and have good reason for riding against the barbarians – we were forced to witness insensate carnage a while ago and may, perhaps, pay them back in their own coinage.'

Dyvim Slorm nodded and swung off his mount. The beast stirred restlessly and drew back the lips of its tapering snout to reveal teeth as thick as a man's arm, as long as a sword. Its forked tongue flickered and it turned its huge, cold eyes to regard Elric.

Elric sang to it in the old Melnibonéan speech, took the goad and the Dragon Horn from Dyvim Slorm and carefully climbed into the high saddle at the base of the dragon's neck. He placed his booted feet into the great silver stirrups.

'Now fly, dragon brother,' he sang, 'up, up and have your venom ready.

He heard the snap of displaced air as the wings began to beat and then the great beast was clear of the ground and soaring upwards into the grey and brooding sky.

The other four dragons followed the first and, as he gained height, sounding specific notes on the horn to give them directions, he drew his sword from its scabbard.

Centuries before, Elric's ancestors armed with *Stormbringer* and its lost sister-sword *Mournblade* had ridden their dragon steeds to conquer the whole of the Western World. There had been many more dragons in the Dragon Caves in those days. Now only a handful remained, and of those only the youngest had slept sufficiently long enough to be awakened.

High in the wintry sky climbed the huge reptiles and Elric's long white hair and stained black cloak flew behind him as he sang the exultant *Song of the Dragon Masters* and urged his charges westwards.

> *Wild wind-horses soar the cloud-trails,*
> *Unholy born doth sound its blast,*
> *You and we were first to conquer,*
> *You and we shall be the last!*

Thoughts of love, of peace, of vengeance even were lost in that reckless sweeping across the glowering skies which hung over that ancient Age of the Young Kingdoms. Elric, archetypal, proud and disdainful in his knowledge that even his deficient blood was the blood of the Sorcerer Kings of Melniboné, became detached.

He had no loyalties then, no friends and, if evil possessed him, then it was a pure, brilliant evil, untainted by human drivings.

High soared the dragons until below them was the heaving black mass, marring the landscape, the fear-driven horde of barbarians who, in their ignorance, had sought to conquer the lands beloved of Elric of Melniboné.

'Ho, dragon brothers – loose your venom – burn – burn! And in your burning cleanse the world!'

Stormbringer joined in the wild shout and, diving, the dragons swept across the sky, down upon the crazed barbarians, shooting streams of combustible venom which water could not extinguish, and the stink of charred flesh drifted upwards through the smoke and flame so that the scene became a scene of Hell – and proud Elric was Black Sathanus reaping awful vengeance.

He did not gloat, for he had done only what was needed, that was all. He shouted no more but turned his dragon mount back and upward, sounding his horn and summoning the other reptiles to him. And as he climbed, the exultation left him and was replaced by cold horror.

'I am still a Melnibonéan,' he thought, 'and cannot rid myself of that whatever else I do. And, in my strength I am still weak, ready to use this cursed blade in any small emergency.' With a shout of loathing, he flung the sword away, flung it into space. It screamed like a woman and went plummeting downwards towards the distant earth.

'There,' he said, 'it is done at last.' Then, in calmer mood, he turned to where he had left his friends and guided his reptilian mount to the ground.

Dyvim Slorm said: 'Where is the sword of your forefathers, King Elric?' But the albino did not answer, just thanked his kinsman for the loan of the dragon leader. Then they all remounted the dragons and flew back towards Karlaak to tell them the news.

Zarozinia saw her lord riding the first dragon and knew that Karlaak and the Western World were saved, the Eastern World avenged. His stance was proud but his face was grave as he went to meet her outside the city. She saw in him a return of an earlier sorrow which he had thought forgotten. She ran to him and he caught her in his arms, holding her close but saying nothing.

He bade farewell to Dyvim Slorm and his fellow Imrryrians and, with Moonglum and the messenger following at a distance, went into the city and thence to his house, impatient of the congratulations which the citizens showered upon him.

'What is it, my lord?' Zarozinia said as, with a sigh, he sprawled wearily upon the great bed. 'Can speaking help?'

'I'm tired of swords and sorcery, Zarozinia, that is all. But at last I have rid myself once and for all of that hellblade which I had thought my destiny to carry always.'

'*Stormbringer*, you mean?' she gasped.

'Of course, what else?'

She said nothing. She did not tell him of the sword which, apparently of its own volition, had come screaming into Karlaak and passed into the armoury to hang, in its old place, in darkness there.

He closed his eyes and drew a long, sighing breath.

'Sleep well, my lord,' she said softly and, with tearful eyes and a sad mouth, lay herself down beside him.

She did not welcome the morning.

The Mercurial Mind of
MICHAEL MOORCOCK

Britain's most imaginative, most original writer of works of fantasy (Science Fantasy . . . Swords and Sorcery . . . Dream Trips . . . what you will – each book is a gem of action, adventure and colourful, kaleidoscopic scenery) is published by Mayflower Books. If you want to escape present-day insanity and discover new worlds follow Michael Moorcock on the voyage of a lifetime. Start here:

Science Fantasy

THE QUEST OF THE DNA COWBOYS	Mick Farren	60p	☐
THE HOLLOW LANDS	Michael Moorcock	50p	☐
AN ALIEN HEAT	Michael Moorcock	40p	☐
THE JEWEL IN THE SKULL	Michael Moorcock	40p	☐
THE MAD GOD'S AMULET	Michael Moorcock	40p	☐
THE SWORD OF THE DAWN	Michael Moorcock	40p	☐
THE RUNESTAFF	Michael Moorcock	40p	☐
ETERNAL CHAMPION	Michael Moorcock	50p	☐
PHOENIX IN OBSIDIAN	Michael Moorcock	50p	☐
COUNT BRASS	Michael Moorcock	40p	☐
THE CHAMPION OF GARATHORM	Michael Moorcock	40p	☐
THE QUEST FOR TANELORN	Michael Moorcock	40p	☐
STEALER OF SOULS	Michael Moorcock	40p	☐
STORMBRINGER	Michael Moorcock	50p	☐
THE SINGING CITADEL	Michael Moorcock	35p	☐
THE KNIGHT OF THE SWORDS	Michael Moorcock	50p	☐
THE QUEEN OF THE SWORDS	Michael Moorcock	40p	☐
THE KING OF THE SWORDS	Michael Moorcock	40p	☐
THE BLUE WORLD	Jack Vance	60p	☐
THE PNUME	Jack Vance	50p	☐
THE DIRDIR	Jack Vance	50p	☐
SERVANTS OF THE WANKH	Jack Vance	40p	☐

All these books are available at your local bookshop or newsagent, or can be ordered direct from the publisher. Just tick the titles you want and fill in the form below.

Name ....

Address ....

....

Write to Mayflower Cash Sales, PO Box 11, Falmouth, Cornwall TR10 9EN.

Please enclose remittance to the value of the cover price plus:

UK: 18p for the first book plus 8p per copy for each additional book ordered to a maximum charge of 66p.

BFPO and EIRE: 18p for the first book plus 8p per copy for the next 6 books, thereafter 3p per book.

OVERSEAS: 20p for the first book and 10p for each additional book.

Granada Publishing reserve the right to show new retail prices on covers, which may differ from those previously advertised in the text or elsewhere.